LOVERS OR
SOMETHING LIKE IT

FLORIAN ZELLER

LOVERS OR SOMETHING LIKE IT

Translated from the French
by Sue Dyson

PUSHKIN PRESS
LONDON

For Caroline

Original text © Flammarion
Lovers or something like it first published in French
as *Les amants du n'importe quoi* in 2003

Translation copyright
© Sue Dyson 2005

This edition first published in 2005 by
Pushkin Press
12 Chester Terrace
London NW1 4ND

British Library Cataloguing in Publication Data:
A catalogue record for this book is available
from the British Library

ISBN 1 901285 52 9

Cover: *The Observer and the Observed No 7*
© Susan Derges
Frontispiece: *Florian Zeller, 2004*
courtesy of Flammarion

Set in 10.5 on 13.5 Monotype Baskerville
and printed in Britain
by Blacketts, Epping, Essex

ïi institut français

This book is supported by the French Ministry for
Foreign Affairs, as part of the Burgess Programme
headed for the French Embassy in London
by the Institut Français du Royaume-Uni

LOVERS OR
SOMETHING LIKE IT

For my brother

Oh! pourtant, pourvu qu'elle m'aime à nouveau pour que je puisse continuer à ne plus l'aimer.

Oh! and yet I just want her to love me once again so that I can continue not to love her any more.

BERNARD FRANK
L'Illusion comique

FIRST SPHERE

1

MY LIFE HAS long resembled a summer that is about to end. It's strange but that's the way it is. Sometimes in these final days, these sombre days, weighed down by a desperately motionless sky, the certainty that the days are approaching when greyness will re-establish its autumnal empire rises up inside me until it becomes dread. Don't you feel that it is already growing cooler?

Today, I feel that I have nothing but my past left to live.

And yet I have not surrendered, I still search for the face borrowed from the tender dreams of adolescence, a face to love. And, with my forehead pressed to the window like a watchman on the lookout for despair, I attempt to picture it.

"Are you afraid of death?"

"Yes, obviously."

2

THE STORY could begin like this: outside O's apartment building, she pushes open the door with a childish gesture, she gives him a discreet sign, a movement of the head that is meant very obviously as an invitation, it must be one o'clock in the morning, they have had dinner together, and Tristan must decide: Are you coming up for a drink? He looks at her in an obscure way, a way she doesn't really understand; she doesn't yet know whom she's dealing with.

They had dinner in an Italian restaurant not too far from her place, they behaved as if there was nothing of consequence going on, in the midst of melons, hams and wine. After dinner, they decided to go for a drink, which was a way of deferring the decision. The uncertainty produces a sort of drunkenness when it is transformed into coquetry.

She lives locally, and he offers to walk her back home. Now they have arrived outside her apartment building, and Tristan once again finds himself in the situation I began with: she pushes open the door with a childish gesture, she gives him a discreet sign, a movement of the head meant very obviously as an invitation, and he must decide: do I go up?

If the story begins at this precise moment, it is because with hindsight I can see the key to everything that is going to follow, the first note in a musical score that is cynical and cruel, but in the end comical.

3

OUTSIDE the apartment building, Tristan thinks of Amélie. He tells himself that he is going to cheat on her tonight, that this will be the first time. Did he really believe, for one day, that he would manage to rid himself of this madness that drives him from girl to girl? In the beginning, perhaps; but beginnings don't mean anything, beginnings lie.

Amélie entered his life as a thief would have done. They met, that's all; he felt a love for her that has remained inexplicable; and now here he is in front of this apartment building, with another girl, and he knows that he is going to cheat on her. It is now a certainty.

Tristan does indeed want to "come up and have a drink". He says so in a neutral voice, so as not to implicate himself too much. He agrees in the same voice he would have used if he had refused, only it's the opposite.

O has already entered the door code for her building, and she goes in first.

4

HOW DID IT happen? He met O for the first time a week ago. They met like thousands of people meet, at an ordinary party. At first sight he found her neither beautiful nor ugly; he didn't even find her nondescript.

Later, he noticed her voice. It was disturbingly reminiscent of that of a girl he had loved. Behind the thirty-year-old self-assurance, you could make out the hesitant timbre of a little girl, a forbidden sensuality. He began to joke, and she to laugh. But all this was just a vulgar pretext: O is not a sufficient reason.

He had known from the start that he would be unfaithful to Amélie one day. All the letters of the alphabet could have been suitable; O just happened to cross his path that night, that's all.

They don't talk as they climb the stairs. They go up three floors. She lives in a two-roomed flat. She apologises for the cardboard boxes, she's only just moved in. While she goes into the kitchen to look for something to drink, Tristan looks around him. Books are piled up on the mantelpiece. There is one with a yellow cover called *Everything is a Sickness*. He thinks about it and tells himself yes, we do not recover from anything. You can die from virtue too.

O comes back. She hands him a glass. She brought this bottle back from Rome, she explains. They look at each other for a brief moment without saying anything. Tristan suddenly has the impression that this silence is shot through with an indefinable nuance, that which distinguishes the blank part in a conversation from the obvious absurdity of all spoken words.

Moreover, what would he have to say to her? He can't lie to himself, he knows why he's come up to her place, and that doesn't merit a discussion. He empties his glass, he would like it to happen quickly now. But she sits down on the sofa and explains to him that she lived in a bigger place before, but that it always smelt of damp, which, in a more general way, is the major problem with the apartment buildings in this neighbourhood ... He isn't listening. He just gives her a smile of agreement, this smile he's dragged around all evening, and which promises that tomorrow his face will be worryingly stiff. He looks back at himself, all evening, manufacturing this grimace, this ignoble insincerity that one detects in a dancer who has hurt her foot, but who must patiently wait for the end of the music. His former fervour and frenzy have been modestly effaced behind little elegant precautions, these precautions that give the feeling that he possesses the power effortlessly to drive things to their worst, this power—from which he attempts to protect himself—to degrade life.

In the middle of a sentence, however, he kisses her. She pretends to be surprised. Out of coquetry again. And out of indignation, signifying that you don't cut her off like that. Then she relaxes, lets herself go.

Afterwards, they make love in a bed.

In the morning, Tristan awakes with an aftertaste in his mouth.

5

HE KNEW from the start that this day would come. For weeks and weeks, he thought of nothing but this. Women in the street had become an unbearable poison, which he had vainly attempted to resist. Did he feel better now? He didn't really know.

Amélie too had known it would be like this from the start. In any event, that is how he interpreted her excessive jealousies. They had walked hand in hand towards this idiotic destination.

Tristan gets dressed again in a hurry while through the curtain he can already make out the possibility of a new day.

O is still in bed. She sees quite clearly that he looks embarrassed, and immediately guesses what that means. She finds the situation comical and disagreeable. Cowardice is a sort of failed confidence, she thinks, an admission of weakness. It seems that women spend their lives hearing men's confessions.

Now, Tristan would like to run away as quickly as possible, discreetly, like a thief who has just seized a piece of the evidence of his own stupidity.

He prepares to leave. He invents a pretext in the modest hope of being believed. He closes the door behind him. Goes down the stairs. Finally arrives in the street. The cool air of dawn. But nothing's any good, it's always the same. Then he takes off into the city, he walks for a long time, but nothing's any good. For it's himself he wants to run away from, and that's impossible.

6

H E THINKS BACK to the day when he met Amélie for the first time. Often, the events of his life are charged with a strange sweetness when he recollects them, an invented sweetness. Often, it is in memory that he seeks his emotions. In a general way, he is obsessed with time. He looks at life trickling between his fingers, he can see that he won't succeed in holding it back, and then he feels a delicious melancholy. The smell of autumn, a sensation of respite.

Amélie appeared one evening, that's all. They made love the very first night. And, a few weeks later, in an inexplicable way, she moved in with him.

Inexplicable, for he had always promised himself that he would remain independent. He desired women too much to live with one of them in particular. Why should it have been any different with Amélie? She had overturned his assurances. With her, he had acted against his principles. He had given her the progressive possibility of moving into his life.

The classic love-stories weren't for him. Maintaining a relationship, living as a couple, being faithful, being subjected to the other person's jealousy, perhaps getting married, and, who knows, one day having children: these outmoded formulae inspired only contempt in him.

He had lived with a woman before, two years previously, but the thing had very quickly turned into a nightmare. Separation had swiftly followed moving in: he had realised that he was not made for living with somebody else. He organised himself so that the women he met did not expect anything from him. This was the sole guarantee of his freedom: the exclusion of all sentimentality. I believe that the idea came back to him often, like an obsession, that life must be exhausted, that you have to feed, as a bulimic would, on everything it contained by way of experiences, pleasures and obscure promises.

He had been a solicitor for only a few years. After performing brilliantly in his studies, he had set up his own chambers, which were enjoying a growing success. But this aspect of life seemed not really to interest him. Women occupied a much larger part of it and had left his name with a reputation for scandal, even immorality, the sort of reputation that people are astonished can still exist today.

But with Amélie, he had undoubtedly sensed that things were going to be different. And yet he had done nothing to prevent the disaster: as he saw her moving in to his life, he had to bid farewell to a part of himself, his life as a libertine, and that seemed to him close to masochistic torture.

7

THEY HAD MET for the first time in the street. Tristan was waiting on the edge of a pavement for the lights to change colour. Suddenly, behind him:

"Excuse me … "

A young woman was standing there, and there was something unreal about her presence. She wanted to know where the Polish Bookshop was. It was assuredly the first time anyone had asked him that question.

"You're looking for the Polish Bookshop?"

"Yes … "

He knew where it was, "I'm going that way", and could perhaps accompany her. She shrugged her shoulders, as if acquiescing, and the lights turned to red. When they crossed, he noticed that she walked so as to step only on the white lines. At one moment she was obliged to take a larger step so as not to lose her game, the last remnants of childhood, the amused corpse of the person we no longer are, and when she turned her head towards Tristan, caught in the act, she started to blush.

They walked side by side to the bookshop, but remained silent. The situation was becoming almost awkward. Words found it difficult to follow the path of feeling. Tristan moved a little closer to her to see her reaction. She was perhaps beautiful. Not with that exhausting beauty that would meet with unanimity, but with an uncertain, fragile beauty. Debatable.

All meetings are improbable in themselves. However, for Tristan, the fact that this meeting took place in the street, made the attraction he had immediately felt for her even more disturbing. Why her? Why her and not another? Why him?

Yet he had done nothing to merit falling in love. Without a doubt it's God's pleasure alone to appreciate the workings of justice.

8

IN GENERAL, Tristan fell in love each time he crossed the road. But this movement, driving him towards women, in reality had nothing to do with a simple quest for pleasure; it derived rather from a permanent harassment of the possibilities, a feeling of jubilation at extending his empire, an empire broader than the empire over others, from an almost tourist-like anxiety.

Women's bodies gave his desires that sublime fixedness through which the forces of youth are pointlessly used up. At twenty-nine, he still had something of the adolescent about him. He was regarded as tetchy, sombre, dreadful; and yet, his beauty aroused a sort of muted cult, and people were easily conquered by this devil who seemed shot through with a strange grace, the grace that makes you forgive everything.

But that day, the first night, it seemed to him that he touched something unique. There, with her offered up to him, he was obliged to undress her, because she would not have done it herself. She did not move, was anxious, waiting for him to take her, for it to happen. And at the moment he withdrew, he had the impression that he spotted tears, tears in her eyes. Had she been crying? Or was it only an impression? Had he hurt her? He might have been annoyed by this kind of sentimentality, but no, he was rather troubled, moved. He realised then, through those tears that he was not certain he had seen, he realised, at the moment when the possibility of suffering had not yet found a way to slip inside her, no crack in the armour, nothing, not a tear, he realised that Amélie belonged to the category of the most beautiful women of all: those who are made of glass. He realised also that this fragility was overwhelming.

Suddenly, his mistresses who shouted out their orgasms and whose faces were deformed by the insistence of pleasure became vulgar, contemptible people. By weeping before him, Amélie had become a child, a child whom he must protect. Against what exactly, he would not have been able to say. But he would have given everything for this woman whom he had known for only a few hours.

Tristan watched her sleeping and, although she could not hear him, he whispered in her ear, telling her that he loved her, without quite knowing what that meant. Without knowing that he had just fallen into an absolute trap, the tenderness trap, and that it was ridiculous, unremittingly ridiculous.

9

THAT'S NOT EXACTLY how things happened. The Polish Bookshop was closed. Amélie didn't display any disappointment. Once again, she shrugged her shoulders. They looked at each other in silence. Now they had to say goodbye. Her body made a surprising movement, the suggestion of a movement, and Tristan realised she was about to leave. Should he hold her back? He wanted to say something to her, but, unable to grasp the unknown element of this moment, he did not know what. Here she is, already thanking him, she is preparing to vanish completely, and, for a reason that escapes him, yes, he would like to hold her back, as he always attempts to hold women back. What would he say to her? At this precise moment, something ought to have been attempted, but hasn't been. So, faithful to the suggestion, she walks away and once again becomes one of those ghosts of women met in the street and who, for the space of an instant, draw all the importance out of the rest of the world.

Did she see it in his eyes? It is impossible to know— impossible to know, consequently, exactly when this story begins. Perhaps it should be taken from the moment three weeks later when she came through the door of an immense apartment, at an ordinary party. Summer dress over soft music. Tristan recognised her immediately, from a long way away, a glass in her hand: the woman from the Polish Bookshop. As for her, she seems to be paying him no attention. He observes her from over there, seeks out her gaze for a long time. She is accompanied by another girl he does not know.

How did things happen next? Today, he can remember only one thing: they left together. If they spoke, what exactly did he say to her? He has forgotten. She, in any case, did not talk very much, and her eyes still escaped him, not because they were fleeing something they could not have borne, but because they seemed summoned by a distant universe in which nobody could join her. When she was asked a question, she took a little time to answer, as if she considered it decidedly strange that this world should sometimes summon her back; then, in a voice that was scarcely there, she answered softly, and you suddenly had the impression that it would have been better to keep silent, not to say anything, to leave her to her freedom, her mystery. She did not express any hostility. No annoyance. She just didn't belong to this world. Her name was Amélie.

After the evening out, they went up to his place. And, in an inexplicable way, a few weeks later, she moved into his life. That's what I know.

10

THE BEGINNINGS of a story about two people often take on the appearance of magic. In reality, this is the weightiest, the most decisive moment. That is why I am beginning with it. For everything is definitively at stake: the reciprocal roles are drawn, the relative strengths are established, a sort of implicit contract is signed between the lovers, and any ulterior challenge to this contract is impossible.

So it is not insignificant that Tristan's initial tenderness should have come from Amélie's fragility. He gazed at her, beautiful and perhaps asleep, yet already this was no longer the anonymous object of a conquest. He was practically certain he had seen her weeping just now. Moreover, her make-up had run a little, he stroked her cheek and a black mark appeared on one of his fingers. This image did not mean anything, but he wanted to give it meaning. For him it was the poetic proof that this woman's tears were in his hands, and that he was there to protect her. What he did not know, was that this black mark was going to serve as the ink for a contract in which it would be written that Amélie would be weak, and that he would be moved by it. It was also written that the weaker she was, the more he would love her.

The following morning, Amélie was looking at herself in the bathroom mirror. She let the tap run to take out her lenses. She must have kept them in all night, and now her eyes were irritated. As she looked at herself in the glass, she noticed that her makeup had run. Never sleep with your lenses in. She looked in the cupboards for some cotton wool to clean her face. That was how she discovered a pot of skin cream, hidden behind some other things. She recognised it immediately, since she had the same sort at home. Who could it belong to? To another woman? The green of her eyes grew troubled. She realised suddenly that she knew practically nothing about the man with whom she had spent the night.

In her mind, that inoffensive pot betrayed the presence at some time of another girl and thus seemed to confiscate her hope of being unique. Were there other women in his life? She had a feeling of disgust as she imagined that she was perhaps only one among others. In a general way, she did not like other women. She feared them, found them wicked, vulgar, stupid, devoid of morals; on this point, we cannot blame her.

What she does not know, on the other hand, is that the black mark that is losing patience under her eyes will serve as the ink for a contract. Where it will be written that Tristan will be suspected of meeting other women, that this will make her sad, and that she will immediately be ashamed of her sadness.

11

THEY SAW EACH OTHER increasingly often. Tristan's friends did not understand why he continued seeing this girl. What's more, he didn't understand it himself. He remembered the look he had directed at her bare shoulder, the evening he had met her for the second time: it was merely a look of conquest, nothing else. The prolongation of such a look normally ends in a bedroom and ends by vanishing first thing in the morning in the memory of one night's love-making. And yet, she was still there. Interminably there. One day, Nicolas advised him to leave her. "She's not the girl for you! You don't love her!" In a way, Tristan saw the true mark of friendship in this piece of advice. For, when a friend doesn't disapprove of a woman, there's a risk she'll become his.

"Why do you say that I don't love her?"

"Because I can see it. You feel some affection, perhaps. But that's nothing, affection. It doesn't last very long … "

Amélie moved in with him progressively. At first it was a few inoffensive objects: a hairbrush, some books, a bottle of perfume. Creams. Then she put a change of clothes in the big wardrobe. And, after a few weeks, the proof of her existence was scattered all over the apartment.

In silence, Tristan was tortured. Each day he buried all the potential lives whose deaths he must accept. He was run through by thousands of contradictory trains, travelling in inverse and opposite directions; he could not work out what he really wanted.

Several times, he'd wanted to stop everything, explain to her that he wasn't made for living in a couple. But these impulses were dispelled as soon as he saw her. For the first time, he found himself weak. When he showed signs of annoyance, it was enough for her green eyes to tremble, and immediately he apologised, took her in his arms. Consoled her. He was a prisoner of his affection, and the more the weeks passed, the more arguments this affection had.

"You won't ever leave me, will you?" she asked sometimes with a disagreeable naivety.

"What?"

"Promise, it's important."

He promised. However, he was permanently filled with the desire to see other women. In fact, what was preventing him from doing so? He did not believe that one person could satisfy all of one's expectations. He had no morals. The only thing holding him back was a sort of fear, the fear of hurting her.

He thought of Ulysses who, foreseeing that he would succumb to the temptation of the sirens, had had his hands tied to the mast of his boat. In the same way, he avoided everything that might have awakened the desire within him to be free and seductive. As for the world, thus revealing its own cruelty, Tristan began to see it as a naked woman, but one he could not touch, an absolute ban, a sort of prison of desire in which he too found himself, bound hand and foot, with a hard-on for all eternity.

His former mistresses did not understand this change. He no longer lifted the receiver when they called, and behaved as if they did not exist. In a sense, Tristan was ashamed. He had even decided to put some distance between himself and Nicolas and the others. Love is a form of isolation, which you experience as a couple. In the street, he was constantly worried about happening upon one of his girlfriends. Amélie laughed, hung on to his arm like a little girl, while he, devoured from the inside, dreamed of escaping from this prison. He knew that if one of them saw him like this, she would laugh fit to burst, and this laughter, even if imaginary, was unbearable to him.

It came to the point where he could think of nothing but other women. Their fantastic bodies. He even found himself following one at random. To feast his eyes, as they say. But this pleasure did not satisfy him. What then? Are we to conclude that Tristan does not love Amélie? What is certain is that affection is an unadmitted detestation of the other person. Sometimes, he became aggressive. Why had she come into his life? And why could he not manage to leave her, take up his former life again, this life that had suited him so well?

One evening, they were at a friend's place. Tristan had drunk a bit and, taking fewer precautions than he ought to have done, he did everything to seduce a red-haired girl even though he didn't find her particularly beautiful. Amélie noticed and wanted to go home. Tristan knew that he could have spent the night with this girl if Amélie hadn't been there. The woman with whom he was living was progressively becoming an obstacle to his happiness; he even came to resent her for existing. That evening, they went home in silence; they went to bed without a word.

A few days later, when he was alone in the apartment, he flew into a black rage for no reason. He then headed into the bedroom and took all of Amélie's things out of the cupboards. His idea was very simple: he would pack her suitcases himself. When she came back, she would find them in the entrance with a note asking her to leave the apartment. He would come back in the evening, she would have gone, and at last he would have his freedom, he would have his joy once more.

When he had finished the suitcases, he calmed down. He imagined Amélie finding them in the entrance. Then, frightened by his own cruelty, he decided to put everything back in place.

Tristan had a volcanic temperament, unpredictable, and, because it generally obliged other people to submit to him, he had always taken that as peculiar to a superior strength. But for the first time, unable to work out what he wanted, he was himself subject to permanent oscillations, and the only fixed point he could precisely designate within himself was this affection, which he took to be a weakness, and which indeed was one.

Woman's vanity is to want to turn man into a monogamous individual, he told himself. Her cruelty is to succeed in doing so sometimes, at the cost of turning him into a fearful child.

12

IN THE STREET, he was more and more attracted by the figures he encountered, and the fact that it was forbidden gave everything he was not experiencing a too-brutal savour. Imagining the gaze he could direct at women, I think of the way a tourist would look at a town. According to the guides, there are a certain number of things to see, monuments, fountains, things that are judged indispensable in order to obtain a general view of the place. For my part, I have resolved never again to linger in towns that I happen to pass through. It is the sole bulwark I have found against the unspeakable vulgarity of tourism.

The visit is a way of reducing a place to its most anecdotal dimension and does not enable one to penetrate its mystery, its subtlety, its share of eternity. I was in Rome a while ago, and I witnessed a scene that seems to exemplify what Tristan perceives. A coach load of tourists drew up in front of the Forum. As soon as they came within range of the monument, they took photos of it without even waiting until they'd got off the vehicle, with a frenzy and a swiftness of execution that were terrifying. What were they afraid of missing to make them act in that way? At the basis of tourism is the fear of missing out on the essential things, not making your journey worth the money. It is moreover for that reason that you obtain a guide in which you find out what you "absolutely" have to have seen. You see one monument after another without ever looking for the emotion; what is listed in the guide becomes the only, the miserable criterion for appreciating beauty. The objective becomes almost to add up the photographs, which will soon become the last pieces of evidence of a microscopic ambition, that of saying: "I've done Rome." Ten photos. And soon: "I've done Italy." Fifteen photos. They make me think of people who read "the whole of Balzac". Some people work all year to give themselves this kind of misunderstanding.

The best thing would doubtless be to let yourself be carried along by a place, to divest yourself of the fear of not being in the right place. In Rome, I didn't see any of the monuments considered vital. I enter each town in a complete submission to chance. Insignificant events decided my path: the emptiness of a square, the silhouette of a woman, the mystery of an alleyway. That is how I was planning to capture fragments of Rome's beauty.

That is how Tristan met Amélie. This meeting is the antithesis of vulgarity: she appears one day in the street, and since then she's been there, in his life. This reality arouses a scarcely-stifled violence in him. He thinks of everything he lacks by being with her, and it is precisely the fear of this lack that you find in his eyes when he looks at the other women walking in the street. It is a tourist's gaze. It is lit up by a vulgar curiosity: he would like to see them naked. Worse, he would like to see himself in the midst of these nude figures, like a tourist letting himself be photographed in front of a monument which, basically, he couldn't give a damn about.

Is this to say that Tristan is vulgar? I would say rather that he is attracted by a certain form of vulgarity, which is always a more or less conscious promise of coitus. More and more, Tristan was thinking of flings with no tomorrow, flings he could easily hide from Amélie. The idea of sleeping with another woman now became a fixation. The woman didn't really matter. The monument didn't matter.

His torments continued until the evening with which this story could have begun. Amélie had left for two days to see her mother in Rennes. Tristan invited a certain O to dinner, a girl he had met at a party a few days earlier. She suggested that they go to an Italian restaurant she knew well.

During dinner, they discussed the things you have to discuss in order to end up shamelessly in bed. The relics of civilisation. Play at being refined, gentle, intelligent. I detest the age I live in.

Later, they found themselves outside her apartment block. She made a movement of her head, a sign to him that was very obviously an invitation. She had already entered her doorcode. She went in first.

13

THE WEEKS SLID away like falling stones. It is now more than six months since Tristan cheated on Amélie for the first time. After O, he met other girls. He saw his former mistresses again. He has resumed his former life. He is learning to lie to the woman he loves, and he is surprised to discover that nothing is easier.

One June day, as he is coming out of the apartment where one of them lives, he walks down the street, in the sunshine, and tells himself that he's happy like this. He has the impression that he has found a way of organising things that agrees perfectly with what he expects from life.

His work as a solicitor takes up a lot of his time. But he feels that with women he no longer needs to seduce, since his professional life gives him precisely that sort of satisfaction. There remains pleasure. Here again, his profession is somewhat useful to him. He very quickly realised the relationship that existed between women and money. What's more, the thing is obvious; take any car: the more expensive it is, the better your chances of finding a beautiful woman in it, and that's quite independent of the driver. Things are the other way round today: in the nineteenth century, it was through women that one gained access to power and money; today, it is through power and money that one may possibly gain access to women.

One other observation: he sees quite clearly that relationships have become impossible. The majority of people look as if they're suffocating. We had to leave the shore of childhood and enter an ice-cold sea. Of course, at the start, we believed there would be a shore on the other side. We were told tales of explorers that nobody took seriously and who, alone against the world, continued on towards the unknown: this was how they had discovered new continents. We wanted to imitate them. We've exhausted ourselves swimming out to sea. One day we realise that there will never be a shore before us, and that there is no foreseeable return to the pretty time of childhood. On that day, we are ready for death. In the meantime, pleasure remains.

However, it is not solely pleasure that explains his attitude, but rather a presentiment of the lack of it. How can he manage this concern with his life as half of a couple? Tristan has rented a studio flat, not too far from his office. Sometimes, he meets a girl there. But in general, he prefers to go to see them. That gives him the option of leaving when he wishes to. And so, the two lives are completely separate; neither of the two can exploit the other. Part-time love. He considers the arrangement perfect.

After a while, however, Amélie's stomach starts to complain. One evening when they're at the theatre, she is obliged to leave the auditorium because of the pain. Tristan waits a while, hoping to see her come back, then attempts to join her outside. Several people in the audience groan; you've a right to complain if you've paid.

Tristan finds the corridors empty. Where is she? He scours the theatre, but she has disappeared. He stays a moment longer in front of the main entrance, then searches the local cafes. Perhaps she's sitting down somewhere, waiting for him ... Still nothing. For a moment, he imagines that she has left and that he will never see her again; at this thought, dizziness overtakes him, an attack of dizziness that, he thinks, he will not survive. Then he pulls himself together, surprised himself by his excessive reaction.

Finally he decides to go back home, and finds her stretched out on the sofa in the living room, groaning.

She tells him her stomach hurts. Tristan asks her, a little annoyed, why she left without telling him. She does not reply and just closes her eyes. Do you want me to call a doctor? She signals yes with a nod, that's all.

The weeks pass, and her stomach is more and more painful. She is eating less and less. She scarcely sleeps at all. She can quite clearly see that Tristan is away more than he was before. One day, she happens upon some papers relating to a studio flat Tristan is apparently renting in addition to their apartment. She dares not ask him for explanations. To her mind, losing him would be the worst thing. Her anxiety about not being up to the mark, being abandoned, tears at the tissues of her belly. As if she knew.

14

ONE DAY, M decided to call Tristan's home direct. In general, she was only supposed to call him on his mobile, never at home. She knew very well that she was exceeding her rights as an occasional lover, but it was precisely for that reason that she had dialled the number, to have her revenge on his change of attitude. For Tristan had changed. They saw each other again, but always for very short times. He never stayed the night at her place any more. Most often, they met during the afternoon, and she knew that this sudden change signified that another woman had entered his life.

The first time she met Tristan, he had explained to her that he could never live with someone. Despite his claims, she was certain that this was no longer the case.

Amélie was in the bath when the telephone rang. She stood up as soon as she heard the bell. As she had put foam in the water, she was covered in a fine layer of soap-suds, and she had to rinse herself before heading for the telephone. She thought it was Tristan, he was supposed to call her to tell her where they were to meet; they were going out to dinner that same evening. She grabbed a towel and headed into the sitting room as soon as she was rinsed off, commenting on her own haste in a loud voice: "I'm coming, I'm coming."

But she came too late. The answering machine had already started up. She could have picked up the receiver, but she did nothing; she remained in front of the telephone, feeling a strange excitement at the thought of listening to the message, without picking up the phone. She was really expecting to hear Tristan. So she was surprised when it turned out to be the voice of a woman, a woman she didn't know. She hesitated for a moment: should she pick up the phone? Her throat tightened. It was a certain M; she was leaving a message for Tristan, suggesting that they meet up one night next week. Amélie picked up the receiver.

"Hello?"

M deliberately assumed an offhand manner and asked her if she could leave a message for Tristan.

"I'm listening."

"Could you just tell him to call me back?"

15

HER STOMACH pains were getting worse, but did not yet prevent her from working. In September, Amélie started her second year at the Jules-Ferry primary school. She was in charge of the two infant years and often came back with anecdotes about her day, about what she had been told by the children, whom she adored.

(Sometimes, in the secrecy of the bathroom, she places a hand on her stomach, thrusting it forward as if she were expecting a baby, and talks to it out loud. She says: "How are you, my love? It's mummy. One day, we shall be together and life will be even more beautiful. In the meantime, make the most of the warmth of my tummy. I've worked hard to make you a lovely soft nest ... " She then looks at her breasts and wonders how they will look on the day she really is pregnant.)

Tristan spends a lot of time observing her. He has the impression that Amélie lives in another world, a world parallel to the one they share. Often, she hums. Her voice is sweetly fragile, and constitutes, for him, the mark of this interior world to which he has no access. She sometimes remains standing up, her forehead pressed to the window like a child looking into the far distance. The precise substance of her thoughts is of no importance for the moment. She loses herself in a dream that belongs to her. And is that not the only thing that really belongs to her?

When she is alone, she spends long periods of time listening to music. Sometimes she dances. At the moment, she often puts on a record of Chopin. She would very much have liked to be a pianist. She closes her eyes, and it is the music of exile that echoes in her head. She sees the Polish plains stretching off into the distance, and, beyond the notes, this secret gently confided: in the end the world contains more tears than you thought.

They sleep together less and less often. Tristan has the impression that she could easily do without sex. And yet, to counteract this distancing on her part, she would like to give him everything, become his mistress too, but she does not know how to go about it, and dares not say anything to him.

Once, they had gone for dinner at the home of a couple they were friendly with. The idea of a "couple they were friendly with" was practically unbearable to Tristan. But the worst was still to come: at one point, the girl turned towards them and asked in a jokey tone when they were planning to get married. Amélie looked at Tristan as if he alone could answer. He then felt an unpleasant awkwardness, then, disguised in a false smile, he reminded them that they had "all the time in the world, no?"

16

M LIVES IN a big apartment. She's just got up. Tristan is still stretched out on the bed. He looks at her from behind. He notes with astonishment that this body still attracts him, after all these nights.

She puts her bra back on. And as if it were of no importance, not even bothering to turn her head, she asks Tristan:

"By the way, what does your wife do?"

Tristan looks at her in admiration, stunned. She asked him this question in a neutral voice, so as to signify her victory more emphatically.

"I'm not married."

"Yes, but anyway, it's the same thing."

"She's a primary school teacher."

M turns round with the sole intention of showing him her amusement. Without really knowing why, she had imagined that she was an "artist". A musician, something like that.

"Do you mean to say you're living with a schoolmistress?"

Tristan shrugged.

"In a way, yes."

She is now in her underwear. She approaches, stands just over him, but without touching him. Tristan detects something in her eyes that resembles hatred. In general, she does not entertain any men in her home. She prefers to go to their place. And yet, since the very beginning of their liaison, Tristan has always come here. They have never gone to a hotel together.

"Why are you asking me these questions?"

"Because it interests me … "

Why had she imagined Amélie as an artist? For her, being an artist is the highest level of personal development. She considers that she herself has no special talent. She would very much have liked to do something with her creativity, but she does not feel gifted. It is a sort of complex with her.

She looks at Tristan, and suddenly finds that he has aged. She has only known him two years, but she can clearly see that something has changed in him. A sort of heaviness. How old must he be? He is still young. Two years ago, he represented a centre of gravity. That's what attracted her to him, this ease with which he drew others to him, the collective fascination he could arouse without effort.

"Do you love her?"

"What?"

Once more he assumes that stern look she knows so well, and which frightens her.

"I'm asking you if you love her, that's all."

"I heard … "

"Well I'm sure she loves you. And as for you, since you don't know how to be disliked … "

His sternness fades away: all that can be made out on his face now is an amused, feminine tenderness.

"Are you jealous?"

He starts laughing. And, as she doesn't know how to react, she pretends to laugh too.

17

AMÉLIE'S EYES are shut; she is fighting sleep. She is telling him that she didn't always want to be a primary school teacher. Tristan passes his hand across her forehead; she has a fever.

"At the start, I wanted to teach French. I even started the course in language and literature. One March, I worked in an institute that gave remedial lessons to secondary school pupils in difficulty. It was their fourth year of secondary school. It lasted a week. You see, it was the first time I had found myself in front of a class. I was a bit nervous. In the daytime, I gave these lessons; at night, I prepared the ones for the next day. Because I didn't remember the syllabus very well any more. I really got involved. On the last day, towards the end of the lesson, I felt a sense of relief. I told myself that everything had gone well. I'd been good enough, you understand? At the time, that was important to me. You see, I thought it had interested them. I sensed a bit of restlessness. I asked what time it was. They replied: "Five o'clock!" So there we were, it was finished. They all stood up. In two seconds there was nobody left. I had left them my number, all of that, just in case they should need it. Then I got my things together, I was happy, and I went off to the staff room. It was there that I walked into the director of the institute. It was horrible. He glared at me, as if to ask me for an explanation. I didn't understand. And suddenly I looked at the clock, and I realised. They had lied to me: it was only quarter past four. They had wanted to get out as quickly as possible. In itself, that wasn't very important, it was even understandable, but I think it was the first time I really understood what it meant to be alone.

"Why are you telling me this?"

"No reason. I don't know. Whatever."

18

TOO OFTEN, Amélie's behaviour made no sense. Her stomach pains were not abating. Tristan blamed himself for not doing everything to make her happy. In May, they terminated the rental on Amélie's studio flat. Once again, he was acting against his principles: even though she had not lived in this studio flat for some time, this was giving their affair an official, provisionally final dimension. And so, as if he had wanted to escape from something that would catch up with him anyway, Tristan suggested looking for a larger apartment. They moved a few weeks later to an *atelier* at 34, rue de Verneuil. The evening they moved in, they invited a few friends to dinner. One of them, Pierre, had just bought a boat called *Lafcadio*. Everyone drank a toast to these two new acquisitions. Lafcadio is also the name of one of Gide's characters in *Les Caves du Vatican*. Pierre recounted the famous scene of the gratuitous act: Lafcadio is on a train taking him to Rome and, without any reason, seized by some indeterminate whim, he decides to throw the traveller he's sharing his compartment with out of the window.

That evening, in his bed, Tristan imagined himself on that train. He then remembered, with a stab of pain, the life he had always wanted to have, this life which, little by little, he was passing by, the adventure, this train of madness which, he no longer had any doubt, would remain motionless at the platform. Amélie was already asleep. He looked at her without knowing what he really felt. Take her and throw her out of the window? All he knew was that he was already beginning to miss his old apartment.

The next day, he went to a bookshop to buy Gide's novel.

He opened it as he had opened the Bible when he was a child, at random, and happened upon this sentence, which left him in an obvious stupor: "Thirty-four rue de Verneuil," he repeated as he walked along; "four and three, seven: the number is good." The coincidence seemed impossible to him. Stupor turned to anguish. Chance seemed to be constructing invisible prisons. He decided not to talk about it to Amélie, who now seemed happy and calm.

But her smile did not last very long. Soon her pains started up again. Something had happened without Tristan realising. Had she caught him with another girl? That seemed unlikely to him. One day, right in the middle of the afternoon, she had an attack. Such a bad one that as soon as he was informed, Tristan took her to see a doctor who found nothing in particular.

"The stomach is a very sensitive part of the body," he explained. "You must not eat acidic things for a while. I shall prescribe you some medication, and if you are still ill in three weeks' time, we shall have to carry out more detailed tests."

Three weeks later, the tests did not give any satisfactory answer. Amélie almost wished they could find an ulcer. For the pain that has no name is even more acute. Analysts concluded that the illness was psychological. Humiliated, Amélie said nothing.

The doctor took Tristan to one side. "She must take care of herself. Does she have problems in her life? Things could get worse ... "

On the way home, they said nothing. Tristan was thinking back to what the doctor had told him. He would have liked to protect her. But from what? From himself? He looked at her out of the corner of his eye. Did she suspect his infidelities? How could she know? These questions went round and round inside his head during the journey. As usual, he drove too fast.

19

THE LIGHTS turn to amber, but Tristan accelerates. Amélie flinches back into her seat and hangs on to the seat belt. They cross the junction at top speed, and a car coming up on the right sounds its horn furiously.

And yet he knows I hate taking this kind of risk, she thinks. A moment's lack of attention can mean death.

A little further, in the rue de Rivoli, another light turns amber, and Tristan still does not brake.

"Slow down!" she tells him then.

Tristan is surprised by the tone of her voice. She practically shouted. The car stops in time.

"Do you want to kill us or what?" she adds, more gently.

He does not answer.

20

SCARCELY have they arrived at the apartment when Amélie goes into the kitchen. She stands there, her forehead pressed to the window, and she gazes into the distance. She feels weak and humiliated. She has the impression that the doctor was talking to her as if she were a madwoman. Soon she will become a dead weight for Tristan. She does not want to go back and see that doctor any more.

Once again, tears come to her eyes. That is why she closes them. She hates herself for the ease with which she starts to cry. She would like to deny everything wholesale. To be strong and make Tristan happy. She is doubtless a little naïve. But who can differentiate exactly between naivety and purity? She has always believed that life would be like a fairy story. And where are they, the castles, the enchantments, and all the magicians?

Today, she knows that he sees other women. Sometimes, she imagines the way in which he might have cheated on her, and the tears come immediately to her eyes. They would first have met at an ordinary party, as thousands of people meet every evening. Then, he would have invited her to dinner, before going back with her to her place. Amélie can see the scene very clearly: he is outside her apartment building, she makes a discreet sign to him, a sign that quite obviously represents an invitation, and she suggests that he should come up and have a drink. All these images turn round and round in her head. She repeats, she repeats the scene to herself to understand from what moment, from what moment he cheated on her.

She thinks back to the pot of cream she found in his

things that first morning. She ought to have listened to the meaning of this clue. She is beginning to detest that joyous animal quality in him, that slightly savage offhand manner to which, she knows, too many women must succumb.

Tristan is standing in front of the kitchen door. Amélie turns her back on him, she above all does not want him to see her like this, full of emotion. He approaches her. Lays his hand on her shoulder. She makes a little movement to escape from him.

"What is happening?"

She doesn't know what answer she should give. Her stomach is still complaining.

"I must take my medicines."

She attempts to move away, but he takes her in his arms.

"What's wrong?"

She feels a ball of sadness deep in her throat.

"I have the impression you don't love me any more," she ends up saying, drowned in her tears.

Then, tortured by emotion, he takes her hands and kisses them.

"You're talking nonsense. You are the most beautiful thing that has happened to me … "

"Thanks for the "thing" bit," she says, with a sniff.

21

S HE CONTINUES to follow the doctor's advice, but she very quickly realises that this doesn't solve anything. She is more and more ill.

Tristan doesn't know what to do any more. So what! Can't he give up the women who surround him? Some mornings, Amélie can't even go to work. The head of the school, who is a former primary school teacher, finds a temporary replacement for her. And so she stays in her bed all day. Sometimes, Tristan has the feeling she is dying.

He has been in his office since the start of the day, and refuses to be disturbed, has stopped picking up the phone, he is absolutely determined to remain alone until he takes an irrevocable decision.

He looks at himself in the mirror, smiles at his impeccable image. In this light, you'd think he was ten years older, it's strange. He's by far the youngest and most brilliant in his chambers—and he knows it. What's more, he detests the people he works with. So why did he choose this profession? Perhaps he could have done great things in life, if he had fought this fear of depriving himself of certain possibilities, if he had agreed to mutilate himself—self-mutilation is necessary, he tells himself in a low voice, but with what?

When he was younger, a student, he had felt the same inability to know what kind of life he wanted. He secretly envied those who, through lack of talent or because of a vocation, no longer asked themselves the question. He had done his studies as one allows oneself to be borne away by a calm current. Nothing other than this indifference had predestined him for law studies, then for the array of qualifications he could boast. He now had respectability and purchasing power. That was fine. Professional success seemed to him the most accessible requirement since basically it depends only on oneself. Nothing was comparable to the torments you could feel when you were with women—and those torments were commensurate with what he had previously sensed within himself.

He told himself from time to time that there was a certain beauty about leading a double life. Yes, a certain beauty. But he could not deny the grotesque worthlessness of his own. Hell! He was living with a woman he could not manage truly to love, incapable of sacrifice he was cheating on her, and he was causing her pain. He lacked love, that was all. He had always dreamed of a heroic life, eventful and passionate, but the age of heroes is now dead and buried.

Love would have been the way out, but that was an old idea, incompatible with the current way the world works. Slowly, the disinterested element has been ousted from our lives. As for the affection that people generally make do with, that couldn't be enough. Nor could tenderness. Tenderness takes the form of love, while being only a caricature of it.

You feel tenderness for a woman when you consider her worthy of being loved—but you don't love her.

22

LEAVE HER? That might perhaps have been the solution. Yes, but causing someone suffering was effectively suffering twice over. It takes so much courage to accept you're going to disappoint the other person. Imagining Amélie in tears was enough to defuse any immediate desire to break up. What would he say to her? That he wasn't happy? That he needed to get his freedom back? And what would he do with this freedom once he'd got it back? Doubtless he'd set off again to conquer life. But what would she have left? Nothing. He had become an element of her identity. Leaving would amount to abandoning a child at the side of the road; cutting off her food supply. At this thought, a shiver of horror ran through him. She was capable of anything when distressed. The strength of the weak is often reduced to this: arousing virtual feelings of guilt in the other person. In any event, the trap seemed permanent.

At one time, Tristan had believed that all the great uncertainties would cease, that his life, freed by maturity, would take on a shape consistent with his desires. Today, he saw things differently. Or, more precisely, they imposed themselves upon him differently. All those difficult years, in his adolescence, those years of nakedness, of doubt and demand, those years of which he retained only an obscure memory of suffering, today seemed to him like the best ones of his life; and conversely, the ones during which he'd been disabled by will, tracking down pleasures as if he had a bad heart, became singularly ugly. He must give up. At that moment he felt sincere disgust for himself, for his life. Yes, he must give up. But give up what?

23

HE FEELS CLEARLY that something in his organisation has collapsed. Before, he went to see women to feed on life, and, in so doing, he was responding only to a fierce appetite, a sort of vital bulimia. Today, things have changed. He knows that the direct counterpart of his pleasure is Amélie's suffering. Thus, this pleasure bears a new responsibility and now leaves him with an aftertaste of debauchery. Sometimes he even finds a woman without really wanting one. As if he were inhabited by a destructive necessity, a kind of vocation for crime. What is he looking for, deep down?

In any event, he cannot recover that jubilation he felt in the early days. He is even a little depressed. Life seems to have slowly evolved towards something more half-hearted.

Amélie is ill, she has dark circles under her eyes, she is weak, sad, on the point of collapse, and he knows he is responsible for it. He has pushed her into these morbid areas where he can love her fully. He realises that he is destroying her little by little, and that she will let him do it.

No doubt intelligence consists of being able to accumulate contradictory ideas, without however losing one's capacity to live, to think, to act. To know, for example, that everything is destined to die, and at the same time believe in the future like a child who does not yet know. But anyway: he cannot continue like this. The two lives he is leading are fundamentally incompatible. Even if he feels incapable of doing so, he must choose between them.

In geometry, a "sphere" is a surface all of whose points are at an equal distance from the centre.

Tristan is imprisoned in a sphere, since all the desirable objects that surround him are at an equal distance from his own self. He cannot decide which he wants most.

This sphere is the figure of modern immaturity. It positions the individual like a child in the belly of its mother, and, through this permanent state of uncertainty, it is our own beginning that we are seeking.

"In the beginning was the Word" wrote St John. *"And the Word was God."* But what is divine about the beginning? A baby is probably closer to God than any man, even a saint. For it is pure potential: it can still become everything, since nothing has yet begun. And modernity, it seems to me, is haunted by the fantasy of keeping oneself in this state of pure possibility. I would like to be able to become everything. Not to close any door on the infinite number of possibilities. We come to desire everything, everything and its opposite. But desiring everything and its opposite comes close to not desiring anything at all, and quitting existence.

We want this woman, and all the others; this life, and all those that are radically opposed to it. We are frenziedly searching for this world in which nothing deigned to become real, the one that precedes birth by a moment—and as this is structurally impossible, we develop an excessive violence against ourselves and against others.

24

H E NOW HAD a desire to leave his office, but he was waiting for somebody called Nicolas Couturier, whom he'd agreed to meet. He was planning probably to take him on in his chambers. Nicolas was twenty-eight; at least that was what his file said. In truth, Tristan found he seemed a lot younger. A sort of innocent freshness radiated from his roundish face. For a strange reason, Tristan found him likeable. And felt compassion for him. He had the same Christian name as his best friend. What's more, these days, pretty much everybody is called Nicolas.

He arrived on time. He was shown into his office. He had a forced smile, that odious smile you are supposed to wear in the presence of those who have more power than you; he was visibly pretending to feel at ease. He shook Tristan's hand with a little too much enthusiasm, but immediately changed his mind and sat down. He thanked him eagerly for this interview. He seemed to put so much heart into his professional life.

Tristan gave him satisfaction on every point. He didn't even attempt to negotiate. At the end, he asked when he could start.

"In a month, as agreed," he replied immediately.

"You're going on honeymoon, I'm told … "

"Indeed. I'm leaving in a week's time. For Brazil."

"Very nice."

He considered him for a long time. He saw clearly that he was experiencing all of this in an atmosphere of joy. After all, a marriage and a new job, that was rather a joyful thing.

What kind of life must he have? He will doubtless go straight back home, right now, and he'll tell his new wife about the interview in detail. "I set out my conditions and the boss didn't bat an eyelid!" She will be happy for him, and he will be proud to feel that she is happy for him. Straight away, the next day, they'll go and buy furniture from Ikea.

Nicolas looked at him respectfully without daring to interrupt his reverie. Very nice, Brazil. Yes, very nice, and the wedding too, very nice. You wear a ring even on the evenings when you go out without her. That's very nice, but it's not for me! The time of forever. You smile so ardently at each other. You forget other people, you even forget other women, don't you? Me, I can't forget. Do you understand? And yet, I have all the reasons in the world for detesting them, the other women, for not respecting them. I know their game, I know what captivates them, the idiots. And what's more, women for what? For their smile? Their breasts? All in all, I really couldn't care less about those few minutes of tensed muscles in bed. I often find them disappointing, vulgar. Degrading for everyone. At least, I don't know. Except why tirelessly repeat this eternal ritual of garments thrown in the air, caresses and the whole procession of false passions? There is something else. And there's her; all this time, she's alone! And waiting for me there. Do you understand the monstrousness? I am like a prisoner of women. Oh, their flat, snow-white bellies, that you uncover on that first evening! And their oh-so-childish, touching navels! Their hands that shake a little when you touch them for the first time! Oh, their sweet distraction when they sense that it's coming! And their scent of lilac! I shall eternally be the son of woman, that's for sure. In truth, I don't like men; for the most part they bore me. What's more, you're no exception. Kindly leave me now, thank you.

Once alone, Tristan sorted out a few matters that had been lying around on his desk, looked at himself in the mirror again and detected, in the very depths of his eyes, a fierce appetite for destruction. Then he picked up his coat and went out. In the corridor, he met one of the solicitors from the chambers, a short, fat, uninteresting man who constantly displayed an ambitious desire to speak with him, and who, once again, held out his hand in a friendly way. Tristan greeted him in a superior manner.

He went to see his secretary to tell her he was leaving. She lowered her eyes to show that she had nothing to say, but that didn't mean she wasn't thinking. Tristan had not forgotten that he had a meeting one hour later. "I won't be back in time; you'll have to cancel it," he said.

He left the office with a certain relief. He started walking without really knowing where he was going. He thought of Brazil. Then Deauville. It was a lot nearer. He was supposed to be going there the following weekend with Amélie. When had he taken that decision? He couldn't remember any more. He had booked an hotel, that's pretty much all he knew. He didn't feel the least desire to go there. However he knew that it would give Amélie pleasure. Basically, it was only for her. And, when he thought about it, Deauville wasn't Brazil; it certainly wasn't as far away.

He had left his car in the car park. So he would go to her place on foot. He didn't like taking public transport at all. The worst, to his way of thinking, was the train. You always end up in the wrong carriage. There's something sacred about stupidity: how else can you explain that fierce desire, when you encounter it, to blaspheme against it and do it in? On the train, the sight of other people is an unbearable sight: they breathe, they don't speak properly and they make noise. You get to the point of understanding the ones who lose control and who, suddenly, turn out to be assassins, killers, murderers: the superb aspiration for calmness, iconoclastic silence. He spared a thought for Lafcadio.

His footsteps led him to the rue de Rome. I say "his footsteps" to leave a place for chance. In reality, if he had left his office it was, without completely admitting it to himself, to go and see A.

Would she be at home? In general, she worked in her apartment. As he climbed the stairs, a doubt struck him: at this hour of the day, she would probably be outside. He was astonished by the sorrow he felt. He liked spending time with her. But he was not deceived by himself: if he wanted to see her, it was above all to allow himself to be persuaded to leave Amélie.

25

A WAS A LITTLE over thirty. She had been seeing Tristan for a while, and I think that she loved him more than she claimed to.

Tristan had an almost brotherly affection for her. He remembered the beginnings of their relationship with great emotion. It was first of all the sex that had bound them together, but very quickly something else had developed between them, a sort of unquestionable complicity. Of course, they did not see each other very often, especially since Amélie had been around, but that didn't change anything about the continuity of their affair.

She opened the door at the very moment he rang the bell. When she saw him, she gave a complicated smile, laden with mysterious thoughts.

"You were expecting somebody else, maybe," he asked with a sombre look.

"No. Come in. I was in the middle of working … "

He wanted to take her in his arms, but she was already moving away. He placed his coat on an armchair in the corridor, close to the front door. She was wearing a summer dress without a bra and walking barefoot. There was a bottle of water in her hand.

"You see, I'm becoming unbearable: I come to see you without warning."

Another complicated smile.

"You were right to," she said.

She offered him a cup of coffee, which he accepted. She could clearly see that something was going on, but she did not absolutely know what. It seemed to her as if he were absorbed in himself.

"Aren't you working?" she said.

"No."

"Oh?"

"You're right, I'm disturbing you."

"No, stay!"

He sat down, coldly.

"You don't look too good … "

He was indeed feeling a profound sorrow, which seemed to spread out inside him, irreversibly enlarging its empire. He didn't look too good? He detested that image: he only respected himself when he was strong. Or, more exactly, women only respected him when he was strong. Strength! It was the only word on their lips. How could you not feel that you must act out the charade of strength so as to be able to possess them? Doubtless they had some regard for other qualities, but what pleased them the most, the thing for which they were willing to lose themselves—which is to say give themselves—was strength, solely the charade of false strength. So you had to speak in a deep voice, in an assured manner, have a stern look in your eyes and broad shoulders, stifle the weeping child within, be unafraid of life, of the future, of everything that, generally, makes them tremble at night when they find themselves alone, and then just see the delight and the abandonment in their eyes! He didn't look too good? Is it even possible, when you're with a woman, to admit that you are the most fragile of men, without immediately losing all her regard for you?

He gave her a smile that was above all suspicion. He sensed however that she was distant, and the attraction one may have for a woman hangs sometimes less on her own qualities than on a feeling of increasing distance, a more reserved voice that prefigures forthcoming loss.

A little while before, he was walking along the street, and he told himself that he had always preferred the night to the day—and most especially this fleeting moment when one passes into the other, gently, with a sort of economy of hues. You would have to have never known childhood in order not to understand the strange fear of evening. And yet with it, the progressive retreat of day brings a sort of relief. We then rediscover a profound mystery: what has happened? The café terraces have suddenly emptied. A new uncertainty reigns in the streets. The traffic is less congested. People are going home—before going out again? We are at the intermission when everyone changes costumes. We know who we were. No-one knows what we shall be in a little while.

In Paris, when night approaches, he is above all impressed by these boulevards full of pointless lights. Or, conversely, those little streets, still cobbled, that you find around Montmartre and which, at this astonishing hour of day, seem to weave conspiracies of silence comparable to those of a beach abandoned by the summer season. The intermission will soon come to an end, so let's go back into the auditorium, for it will soon be dark.

A doesn't know what to say. She's holding her cup of coffee in both hands. As for Tristan, he is gazing into space with a little too much complacency: she has visibly ceased to exist for him.

"What's wrong?"

"I like the night-time, that's all."

She produced a smile that made an effort at indifference. There was something profoundly touching about its lack of success.

"Yes, I only like the night-time," he went on.

"Winter nights, when it rains and there's nobody about."

"What are you on about?"

"Or else those nights when you feel alone and when you're going to pick up a girl off the kerb. That's how we met, isn't it?

She looked at him for a moment without managing to work out if he was joking or not. It wasn't boredom, or indifference. But a violent form of despair that, like an over-intense light, reveals only the foul reality of each thing—the shadow projected onto a white wall.

To change the subject, A told him about the article she was in the middle of writing. It was the portrait of a writer who had just died, a certain Philippe Soti, a brilliant poet but completely unknown.

"Soti was a little embittered," she explained to him. "I must say he was practically forgotten. In his last years, he decreed that he wouldn't accept any more visits from readers. As if he was punishing them because their numbers were dwindling as time went on. Out of compassion, his wife went and rang the doorbell from time to time … What do you think?"

"Nothing."

"Aren't you listening to me?"

"No."

A got up suddenly, furious. She'd had enough of this. He'd come to see her without warning and was playing the madman. Really, it didn't amuse her one bit. Now, if he would let her, she would like please to get back to work. She had already fallen behind today. And, although he might prefer winter nights, they were still slap-bang in the middle of the day, a summer's day to boot, and she had to finish her article.

He looked at her sternly. He approached her and stroked her cheek; she was on the defensive.

"I love you," he told her then.

She seemed surprised. So did he. He had never told her that before. It had popped out of its own accord. At the same moment, he realised that this phrase didn't mean anything. She stayed stock-still in front of him, seeking the reaction that ought to go with this kind of declaration.

"What are you playing at? Ever since you came into my apartment, you've been talking rubbish!"

Tristan stood up suddenly.

"Are you going?"

He didn't answer and headed for the way out, with an elegant step that nothing seemed to be able to touch.

"You're mad."

He closed the door behind him, and A smiled, as if she knew he was planning to come back.

Twenty seconds later, the doorbell rang.

Tristan was waiting on the landing and felt a bit ridiculous. What indeed was he playing at? He rang a second time. She didn't come. Why is she taking so long? For a moment, he thought she was going to leave him outside. His admiration for her doubled.

He thought over what he had said to her, concerning the girls you could pick up off the street. He has always felt something strange, a sort of instantly-condemned attraction, when faced with a prostitute. In a certain way, he feels the same thing for these women he sees regularly and whom he politely calls his mistresses. But didn't I, for a time, have a happy childhood? And how have things turned towards concreted streets without grass and without repose? I can still remember the magic carpet on which my hopes of love flew. The sad thing is that this past of beauty now fuels my scepticism, the certainty of irrevocable loss.

He was still on the landing when he at last heard footsteps heading for the door, which opened. A was naked. He gazed at her for a long time: she really was beautiful. She took his hand, led him into the sitting room and, once she was clasped to him, spoke in his ear: "Me too."

It took a brief moment for Tristan to realise what she was talking about.

26

THEY MADE LOVE in the sitting room. A seemed driven by a real passion. But Tristan was astonished by the absence of happiness. He could still think rationally: looking at her, contemplating himself in the loving arms of a magnificent woman, but that would have been only a happiness born of self-esteem.

It was not sensual pleasure he had hoped for, that sensual pleasure which could have torn him away from Amélie and make obvious the separation and the joy that would have succeeded it. He was already beginning to regret his behaviour. He was in the process of breaking everything, like those clumsy children who don't yet know how to play the violin.

She was now still pressed against him. A lover's sweat lay on her thighs. Tristan did not know what to say and felt a certain embarrassment, which gave him the opportunity to realise that this was the first time he had felt ill at ease with her. But was this really the same woman?

It seemed to him that he had just opened doors he would have preferred to leave closed, and he knew at that moment that things were going to be impossible. The atmosphere was icy. What did I come here for? he wondered.

She got up, went away for a moment and came back with cigarettes and an ashtray.

"Do you want one?"

He was astonished by her tender smile. So she was that far away from what he himself was feeling at the same moment. In that smile, you could even detect an air of triumph, which shocked him and gave his regrets a more concrete aspect.

"No thanks, I'm going to have to go back to work."

She looked at him, her eyebrows arching.

"To work?"

He got up. She remained silent, dropped her packet of cigarettes and assumed that haughty air he liked so much.

"Can I ask you a question?"

He turned towards her.

"What?"

"What exactly are you expecting?"

"I don't know what I'm expecting, exactly."

She got up too, furious again. Walked as far as the door, which she opened wide. And signalled to him with a movement of the head, a movement that quite clearly represented an invitation.

"Get out of my apartment. And, while you're at it, get out of my life!"

She slammed the door behind him. He remained in the dark for a moment. Really, women understand absolutely nothing, and that is why they are beautiful. He hesitated: ought he to ring the bell again? Then another torture began, the torture of doubt: when all was said and done, didn't he love her a little bit?

He went down the stairs with the same uncertainty with which he had climbed them, thinking of those white sea-shells he'd collected sometimes on the beach when he was a child: you could take them a long way from the sea they'd been removed from and yet still hear it, still hear the din and the death-throes of the waves.

27

H E STOPPED OFF at his studio flat to take a shower, which didn't make him any more cheerful, then he went home. It started raining the moment he entered their apartment building. Amélie was in the midst of taking a bath. He kissed her on the forehead. He was all too aware of the ridiculousness of the situation.

It seems to me that any person, whatever their power or purity, is always subject to an inner force that, underneath, secretly forces them beyond what they are, and this movement can only be reversed when they become disgusted with themselves. As if, by abasing yourself, you could measure the correct height of the person you wanted to be. Tristan was at that point: more than the situation, it was above all himself he thought ridiculous. He really no longer had a choice: he must get an overall view of his life again.

He stretched out on the sitting room sofa. The bathroom door was open and he could hear sounds of water. Tristan pretended to ask himself the question again, but he knew now that he was going to leave Amélie. He couldn't see any other solution. On the other hand, he had no idea how to tell her. He tried to imagine the situation. What would she do? Where would she go? He bitterly regretted having terminated the rental contract on the studio flat she'd been living in before she met him. Things would have been easier.

How was he going to tell her? He would leave her in the most dignified manner possible, without cowardice. For acts of cowardice are like reflexes in moments of breaking up: they appear with the innocence of a draught.

Tristan observed the movement of his thinking and was

surprised by how far ahead of reality it was. Thus, in the abstract world of ideas, he was already separated from Amélie. In truth, like so many others, he regularly adopted this dangerous and self-satisfied attitude towards everything that happened to him: he was present at his own life and was its most faithful spectator. He lied to himself to detect in advance the configuration of the choices he must make. He claimed that he had made his mind up to leave her, whereas he was still drowned in the darkest of uncertainties. He dressed up what he thought, like somebody sensitive to the cold, to attempt to understand what he would be exposing himself to if ever he came to really think what he claimed to think—in short, he was no further forward than at the start of the day, and he detested himself for this weakness.

28

AMÉLIE CAME into the sitting room. She was enveloped in a large white towel. Her hair was wet. She was laughing. And that laugh stabbed right through Tristan's heart.

"I look like a dog," she said.

He thought then about what he was going to say to her and felt a physical pain. When all was said and done, he would not have given her much.

"Did you have a good day?" she asked him.

"Nothing special. Is your stomach all right?"

She shrugged her shoulders a little, then went into the bedroom to get changed. He followed her and went into the bathroom. She was talking to him about her pupils. One of them had brought a box of matches, which had livened up the entire school playground … Tristan listened distantly. He sought out phrases. Suddenly, he encountered his own face in the mirror and, once again, detected in it a fierce appetite for destruction.

Amélie was now standing behind him, and when she noticed his expression, she started in fright.

Sometimes he has access to a very sombre part of himself, to an excessive violence with which he could kill, annihilate. But, even if these impulses partially escape from him, he knows that you can also elevate yourself by violence. Certain mystics will say that, even in the case of God, it's not in your little velvet intimacy that you may have an intuition of his presence, but in the extremity of your frenzied moments, those regions laid waste by sobs, by humiliation.

"What's wrong?"

Tristan gets a grip on himself, turns towards her and takes her in his arms. He feels incapable of hurting her. He thinks again about that little woman he met one day in the street, at the Place Saint-Sulpice, this woman of his heart. She arrived in the May sunshine, like a miracle. That day, she was wearing blue with a high neck, and a hair slide holding the right side of her hair. Remember that moment of the year when women are in harmony with the climate and rediscover impulses to be naked, those bare shoulders, the napes of those necks, those dazzling May smiles. What is beauty? Discretion, Amélie would reply. Yes, but when discretion itself becomes discreet, when it softly vanishes behind the boldness of femininity: do you know where the Polish Bookshop is? Tristan looks back at that moment as one of the most beautiful in his life. How could he have let things fade to this point?

He looks at her for a long time. He remembers all of their affair, this affair he was going to bury once and for all just a minute ago. Amélie is standing behind him and their past processes across her brow: he gets to the point of perfectly confusing memory with feeling.

She does not understand what is going on inside him. So she asks him the question again, a little awkwardly:

"What's the matter?"

"I just love you, that's all."

She looks at him, full of emotion.

If he says that he loves her, why does he see other women? And how can she tolerate it? If she had any courage, she would leave. But she knows quite well that she will never leave. She loves him so much that she prefers to be with him, whatever the price, and even if she has to pay for it with the esteem she has for herself.

He holds her tightly in his arms, moved by her beauty.

Now that he is with her, he feels clearly that he is incapable of leaving her. He is too attached to her. "I can't live without her," he thinks, playing out the charade of love for his own benefit, excited by this diverting show. "I love her."

At this moment, he has completely forgotten the rest. He has forgotten that anguish of passing life by, that anguish which drives him from woman to woman—the anguish of death. You may find him ridiculous today. But who can lay claim to more generosity towards his own torments? He puts real zeal into his collapses, into his uncertainties, he seeks in his frenzied moments something that will divert him from his final implosion. The certainty that he's going to have to destroy and destroy and destroy. Because that's the price of salvation.

At this moment, he has only one thing in his head: not to cause Amélie any more suffering, to deliver her from the tyranny of doubt. He tells himself that she's the woman of his life. Which unfortunately is not sufficient to make her unique.

"Do you think you'll be feeling well enough to go to Deauville?"

She says yes with a nod of the head. But what she doesn't know is that in agreeing to this journey, it is her death, it is her death alone that she has just agreed to.

Suddenly, a violent feeling of dizziness passes through Tristan: the image he has before him, that of the woman he thinks he loves, appears to him as if lit up by the bluish filter of nostalgia. Right in the middle of this tender impulse, he is overcome, as if he were getting a head start on the indisputable passing away of things, by the feeling of their terrible fragility, their imminent flight.

And then Amélie's face takes on the look of those photographs of the departed that people take out after the event, commenting in a low voice: "This one was taken just before!"

SECOND SPHERE

1

WE NOW SEE HER there, in that unknown space; she has moaned softly, but hasn't yet opened her eyes. She isn't really sleeping, yet she can't say where she is.

Then, suddenly, she opens her eyes. She feels a little cold. The wind is making the white curtain dance. She gets up silently and goes to close the window. She sees the sea stretching out before her, and the pallor of the sky seems to indicate that it is still very early. She turns round: Tristan is stretched out on his stomach. There's a pillow over his head, so that you can only see his body. He's still asleep, she tells herself before lying down again.

Normally, in Paris, Amélie always gets up first, and that is tiresome for her. But today it's different: she is happy to be with him in this hotel, in Deauville, and to be able to take advantage of the early morning.

She even feels a real joy at the thought of not having to go to work. Her stomach pains make her days unbearable. But that's not all: in an unexpected way, she senses that she has less and less patience with the children. And yet she loves their universe, their games.

Last week, one of her pupils wanted to talk to her after class. He looked at her with surprising concentration. He had a question. "Mummy says that God isn't in Heaven, but inside me, in my heart … " Amélie hadn't wanted to contradict his beautiful certainties. "Yes, He is in everybody's heart." A look of panic appeared on his face. "So when I eat peas, do they fall right on his head?"

She hesitates to wake Tristan. Several times during the week, she had to leave the classroom. The pains in her stomach are sometimes so strong that she has to sit down and press her hands on her stomach; she can't do that in front of the children. That's why she goes out into the corridor, near to the little coat-racks. Once, the head found her in this position. "Is something wrong?" He looked at her with gentleness. She would have liked to confide everything in him. But the shame of her weakness prevented her. She apologised, she just had a few pains, but it was nothing. He understood, but the children mustn't be left alone in a classroom. "An accident can happen so quickly!" She stood up and, biting her lip, went back into class.

2

AMÉLIE GOES onto the terrace. She tries to remember last night's dream, but in vain. Down below, on the beach, a few people are walking, and a red stag beetle is buzzing like an engine acros the sky. Last night, she told Tristan that, when she was little, she came to Deauville to stay at her aunt's house. She spent two summers on these beaches, a long time ago. She remembered the long afternoons in the sun, the coloured parasols, the death-throes of the waves. She had been happy, perhaps.

Of course, with time she had only diffuse memories of those holidays, but certain sensations remained intact, like the one she had, once, offshore from the beach. Her uncle had taken her out on his windsurfing board. She hung on to the back and, sliding over the water, she let herself be pulled along for quite some time. When the sand was no more than a white streak on the horizon, she had thought about letting go of the board to see what would become of her. Quite simply let go and drown, to see who would come and find her, save her. She didn't have the courage, and returned to the beach, disappointed with herself.

Later, she had felt the same need to fall. To lose herself, always to lose herself so that somebody would come and save her. As if, tirelessly, she wanted to assure herself that she was not alone—which is no stupider than praying.

When she met Tristan, she immediately wanted him to take her offshore, right from the first night. Since then, she's been drowning every day.

3

BEFORE HIM, she had only loved one man. What's more, she was no longer sure now that she had really loved him. His name was Pierre. At that time, she had just arrived in Paris and was working in a bookshop to pay for her teaching course. Pierre came in regularly to buy books. He seemed older than she was, perhaps thirty, but that hadn't removed any of his timidity.

"He never talks, your lover," Cécile said to her one day. Cécile was the girl who worked with her in the bookshop.

"Who are you talking about?"

"Who do you think? The guy who's just left … "

Amélie stopped, embarrassed.

"Why do you call him that? I don't know him."

"But surely you can see he only comes to see you? He pretends to look at the books, but it's you he's watching."

"No, really … "

"I promise you," she said.

In the days that followed, Amélie thought about this again. She knew nothing about this man, she didn't find him particularly attractive, but the simple fact of feeling she was being watched intrigued her. Curiously, she couldn't understand why anyone could be interested in her. Up to then, she had passed through the world like a ghost; she had been transparent for the majority of men. She was pretty, but had always found herself in situations where other girls were getting all the attention. For example, she'd reached puberty very late. She still looked entirely like a little girl when the others were already beginning to look like women. Her entire adolescence had been marked by this distance.

She hadn't really suffered because of it, but she had lived through this period without completely investing in it emotionally, practically indifferent to boys, then to men.

That was perhaps the origin of her horror of putting herself forward, feeling she was being looked at. When she gave her remedial lessons for the failing secondary school pupils, she had felt an excessive awkwardness at the thought of climbing onto a dais, writing on the blackboard while knowing she was being observed from behind. Several times she had caught herself pulling down her pullover to hide her backside.

Initially she had wanted to teach French. Then she realised that she was not cut out for standing alone in front of thirty pairs of eyes that would judge her without the slightest scruple. That is no doubt why she decided to become a primary school teacher. The children, at least, would never subject her to such tortures. Yes, she loved children because, when she was with them, she always had the feeling that she was invisible.

4

FOR AS LONG as she can remember, she has always been afraid of drawing attention to her image. When she was little, coming back from school, she had to pass the terrace of a café, adjoining her own house, and she found this unbearable. There were always lots of people there and, each time, she walked faster so as not to be seen. But she had this feeling of anxiety even when she was alone: wherever she was, she could feel a persistent gaze upon her. And without really knowing why, she guessed that this gaze belonged to her mother.

Françoise met the man who was going to be Amélie's father one summer, when she was working in a restaurant. She was still a student, and the young Austrian, who was on holiday in Paris, undertook to seduce her. They spent the whole month of August together. Then he went back to his own country. They wrote to each other for several weeks, but ended up forgetting each other.

The following year, Thomas came back to Paris: the company he was working for had given him a one-year posting to the capital. As soon as he arrived, he got in contact with Françoise again, and their affair recommenced. A few months later, she accidentally fell pregnant. She hid it from Thomas until the "problem" became obvious. He then asked for another post in the French subsidiary and was able to stay with Françoise. He married her.

In reality, he had never planned to live with her; he hadn't even thought about it. But when he learned that she was pregnant and that it was too late to think about an abortion, he realised there was no other option. The first months were happy, but very quickly he had the feeling that he had fallen into a trap, of not having really chosen the life he was leading. He met other women.

When Françoise discovered this, he had just had the offer of a job in Germany. He did a runner with his new companion and settled there.

After he left, Amélie's mother fell into a violent depression that never ended. She threatened several times to commit suicide, even several years afterwards. Once, coming back from school, Amélie had found her stretched out in the living room, looking dead. She had mixed alcohol with prescription drugs. After shaking her in vain, she rang the neighbouring woman's doorbell and the woman rang for an ambulance. Amélie's mother remained in hospital for several days.

For years, her mother had repeated to her that she was the only thing left to her in the world, in the incessant vein of a long lamentation.

Amélie didn't meet any boys. She even manifested a certain contempt towards them. Showing any interest in them would have been betraying her mother, who didn't want to hear a word about men. No dispute was possible. No betrayal. Amélie was living under the despotic reign of her mother's grief.

5

IT'S EASY to understand why she was particularly troubled by this man who came into the bookshop with the sole intention of looking at her. There was something touching in the timidity of this stratagem. She had been working for just a month when Cécile remarked that Pierre didn't seem as interested as all that in the books. She wanted to know what his name was.

He came back into the bookshop a week later, flicked through a few books, but didn't buy any. What did he do in life? She attempted to imagine what he was.

"In my opinion, he doesn't work," Cécile said. If not, he wouldn't come right in the middle of the afternoon.

Amélie thought often about what she would leave behind her, if she came to die. Who would come and weep at her tomb? It was no good listing the names of the people she knew, all she could see were her mother, her aunt, perhaps a few close friends.

"Have you ever imagined your death?"

Cécile shrugged her shoulders.

"My death? No."

Now she would die in an accident. While crossing the road, for example. Something that was no use to anybody. At least her death would have the pointlessness of her life. You could see a certain coherence in it, in default of detecting a little beauty. But coherence is still a meagre consolation.

Who would come to weep at her tomb?

Right then, an accident. Just like that. Gratuitously. Or maybe in the middle of the night, at her aunt's perhaps. She would be in her bed. For some obscure reason, she couldn't get to sleep. Then, suddenly, she'd feel an excessive anxiety all over her body, plus a multitude of little burning points on her chest; she would receive a burst of murderous gunfire: her hands would tremble for a short moment, before falling calmly alongside her body. She would die without a sound, like those who do not have the privilege of being loved.

"Me, I often imagine my funeral. And I find it intolerable to realise that there will be practically nobody there."

Cécile smiled because of the word "intolerable". What does it change whether there's anybody there or not? Once you're dead, you don't ask yourself that kind of question any more. It's for the others that it's difficult.

Amélie didn't agree. She could imagine the scene perfectly: she sees her body in the coffin. In the distance, you can hear the organ. And above all, around the box, a few people are weeping with dignity, in silence. At this sight, a powerful emotion overcomes her, and the tears come to her eyes—the emotion of knowing that at last someone misses her. You can't survive except through the grief you leave behind you.

That day, she almost came up and spoke to him. She couldn't start with too mundane a phrase, like: "Can I help you?" Or "Are you looking for anything in particular?" What was needed was a more penetrating hook. She had observed that he had bought books of poetry several times. "So, you're interested in poetry." Yes, that might give rise to an interesting discussion. But she'd have to wait for the opportune moment, not spoil this chance. And then, maybe he had no desire to talk. What's more, he was already heading for the way out. Yes, it was already too late to speak to him. In one sense, so much the better. The next time he came, she would talk to him. Yes, the next time, definitely.

6

H<small>E DIDN'T</small> come back. She waited hopefully for him for several weeks. She felt a bit ridiculous: she didn't know him at all, but she was convinced she was going to have an affair with him. It was the first time she had felt that kind of thing. She could see him already, on the day of her burial, sobbing as he bent over the coffin. But Pierre never came back.

What's more, she had no idea of his real first name. She had decided he would be called Pierre because after all he had to be given a name. She also invented a story for him, a past, some regrets. After a certain time, she forgot the features of his face, the way he dressed, the colour of his eyes. She came to doubt if she'd ever even seen him. Pierre had become a blurred image representing the love she would have liked to have known. She told herself that he must exist somewhere, this person made for her. And that with a bit of luck, this time, they wouldn't miss each other. She waited.

Let's understand each other properly: she had not fallen in love with a stranger. She had simply discovered the possibility of love. During her entire adolescence, she hadn't been looked at. And, in her imaginary world, man was the being through whom distress came. But suddenly, through the gaze of a stranger, she realised that she could interest men. She also realised that she liked it. At the same moment, she became beautiful.

She waited. It's always the waiting that creates events, never the other way around. She had a desire to love. She had a few affairs, but they were always disappointing. The men she met were never up to the mark. They had a cruel lack of ambition, were content with little, and she fled from them very quickly. That was her way of not taking the risk of falling in love with an imperfect being.

For several years, her life remained in this state. She was convinced that this was a slow preparation: everything she was experiencing was leading her progressively towards a destination she did not know, but to which she aspired. She walked. Each day she walked in the Paris streets. I don't know what she was looking for exactly. No doubt she was making progress in the preparation of her wait. Her route was never really the same: insignificance altered it for no reason at all, a sunny spell, a greater feeling of liveliness in one street than in another, a shop window, a couple kissing. What was she thinking of during these walks?

She was afraid of growing old, of passing life by, and I think that in walking, she was tirelessly attempting to evacuate these pesky thoughts that attack the last childish hopes, our kingdom that is full of holes, through which life flows, fugitive, immaterial, through which, grown liquid and lukewarm, flow the dreams of days gone by that made us believe in beauty.

That day, she was walking along the Seine. She was following a man she had noticed just before. He walked swiftly, sometimes slowed down, almost came to a stop, then set off again. And what if it was he, say, the man who was waiting for her, what would she do? She wouldn't even dare go and talk to him! As with Pierre, she would let him leave the bookshop, she would transform him into a dream that she could tame, but that would be all, there would be nothing real about it. She came still closer to him. Over the past few days, the feeling of loneliness had become as heavy as steel. She told herself sometimes that she was condemned to remain alone, isolated. The obsession with her own death testified to that, the fear of not being missed by anyone. She had always believed that her life would take on its real meaning once she was dead.

She continued to follow the stranger, as if to conjure this abominable promise. Should she speak to him? Just to prove that she was capable of doing so! They crossed a part of the Latin Quarter. There was nobody else in the street. The entire city was theirs alone. She wasn't the sort to speak to someone she didn't know. On the Place Saint-Sulpice, he stopped at the pedestrian crossing. She caught up with him and at last dared to ask him a question, the first one that came into her head. Do you know where the Polish Book-shop is?

7

S HE IS STILL on the terrace, watching the beach, and she remembers their meeting. She couldn't have imagined, that day, that two years later she would find herself in a hotel room in Deauville with him.

She had contempt for easy women. And yet she had found herself at his place the very first night. He lived in a big apartment beside the Seine. Anyway, it wasn't really the first night. They had seen each other again at a party, by chance, a few days afterwards. She recognised him immediately, but didn't dare speak to him. Occasionally she got faces mixed up. They observed each other in silence for a while, then he approached her. That same night, she found herself at his place.

In the sitting room, he served her a glass of wine. She explained to him why she had chosen to work with children. As he listened to her, he looked at her insistently, as if he were searching for something precise in her.

They made love. It was the first time she had gone to bed so quickly with someone she didn't know. In general, the men she met became discouraged rapidly: they waited a few days, and then realised they weren't going to get what they wanted. She detested people looking at her naked. Her image belonged to her, and she could not bear the thought of sharing it. However little they might take, she felt robbed, dispossessed.

She liked to look at herself in the mirror. It was if she were drawn irresistibly to her image. And yet, she didn't consider herself beautiful, she didn't like her body. But it was like a delicious session of humiliation.

Tristan kissed her first in the sitting room. She wanted to make it last as long as possible, as if to postpone the moment when she would be naked before him.

"You don't close your eyes when you kiss me, do you?"

"Neither do you," he replied softly.

"I was checking, that's all. I'd prefer you to close them. It's more exciting."

Her modesty had nothing to do with timidity. Even after several nights, she would still be ill at ease. In the morning, when she wanted to get up to get dressed, she would ask him to close his eyes once again. He would do so, with tenderness. Then she would get up and gallop to the bathroom.

"It's more exciting?"

He was already starting to undress her. She trembled slightly. She didn't move, she was in the place where he had put her.

"Don't you trust me?"

"Yes. It's just that I'm not used to finding myself in the arms of someone I hardly know."

She was now naked before him, stretched out on the sofa. She kissed him so that he couldn't stand back and view her from a distance. She hadn't imagined that they would stay like this, in the sitting room, in the light. She held him even more tightly, making her kisses into the accomplices of her modesty.

What could she represent for him? Practically nothing. While as for her, she didn't do things lightly. He must understand that she was really giving herself. But you can't demand of someone that, from the first night, he's paralysed with love. Suddenly, she was afraid of heading offshore all on her own.

8

SHE TURNED her head: Tristan was still sleeping. She found him strange, more sombre, more distant, and his change of attitude frightened her. During the journey, the previous evening, he had said practically nothing. She breathed deeply, then closed the window behind her. She sat down on the edge of the bed and looked at Tristan for a long while.

Suddenly, the memory of her dream came back to her, but it was a tenuous memory, on the verge of fading away. She had dreamed of two lovers, who had gone off on their honeymoon to Brazil. Someone had told them that it was "the most beautiful country in the world". They are in a taxi there. The driver stops at the kerb and asks his customer if he'd mind putting the envelope he's holding out to him into the post box that stands just in front of him, on the pavement. He agrees, gets out of the car, and in the time it takes him to post the envelope, the taxi has disappeared. With his fiancée.

Amélie is frightened by her dream. It must be horrible, she tells herself, to go off on honeymoon and lose the one you love. She has heard tell that tourists are frequently kidnapped like this for prostitution. Sometimes they're found completely drugged in a bordello somewhere in the country.

Then she gets up. Once again, she almost wakes Tristan. She would like to tell him her dream. She knows that he won't wake up for a while yet. She doesn't want to mark time while she waits for him. That's why she gets dressed and decides to go downstairs. She could take advantage of this moment to go for a walk on the beach. She closes the door behind her, trying not to make a sound; suddenly she has the feeling that she is seeing Tristan for the last time.

9

SHE REMEMBERS the first months of their affair. She was so happy that often in the morning, when she woke up, she forgot who she was: for a very short time she remained between two worlds, the dream world she was leaving, and the one she lived her life in, which she must violently rejoin, and in this delicious uncertainty a multitude of anxieties were falling over each other. Then suddenly, reality stopped hiding from her. She saw Tristan beside her, and she felt unspeakable relief and happiness. She had not had a clue that anyone could be so happy. The world scarcely mattered to her. The world could die.

Sometimes, she found herself alone in Tristan's apartment, which wasn't yet hers, but which, suddenly, became a little theirs. Then she would put on some music and dance in the big sitting room. She blew kisses through the window at all the minuscule passers by who were walking along the Seine. She scolded the sofa cushions as if they were their children. They just wouldn't stop squabbling at the moment! She didn't know what was happening to them! Fortunately, they would soon be off to spend the holidays with their grandmother! She regarded herself as a little idiotic, but it was so good to be idiotic, as long as you were alone, and it wasn't for too long.

For the first time in her life, she no longer had a desire to be invisible. On the contrary, she wanted people to look at her. On his arm. When they were out walking, she stared at people to check that they had clearly seen that they were in love, that it was undeniable. Had someone asked her if she believed in happiness, she wouldn't have hesitated for a single second. Sometimes, when they met up with friends at a party, the two of them danced together for a long while. Alone, the world reduced solely to their entwined bodies, ignoring everything but the music, this time it was a waltz, a friend's wedding, they spun round and so did their heads, and she felt beloved, determined hands clasping her back and guiding it towards what seemed to her to be happiness, but suddenly she was afraid: what would remain of this embrace when the music was over? And then she remembered, her head flung back, almost looking at the ceiling, drunk, he had promised, they had eternity before them, she remembered, the world was their oyster.

Yes, that is the comical illusion of new lovers: like children, they speak of eternity; like bad poets, they believe in the power of what they are saying; and like us, they drown in the saddest form of cowardice, banality.

10

ONE DAY when she was walking near the Odéon, she spotted Tristan in a restaurant. He was with a girl she didn't know. A lump came to her throat. But she didn't dare go and see him.

All that day, she thought about this unknown girl. Who could she be? Amélie had been with Tristan for practically six months. She already spent most of her time in his apartment. Sometimes when she came back to fetch things from her studio flat she had the strange sensation of no longer being at home. In truth, she had a permanent desire to be with him. And it seemed to her that nothing could ever attenuate the violence of that desire. Ever since she was small, she had been searching for an absolute; at last she had found it.

Her great fear was of being abandoned. The ghost of her mother came back to haunt her affair each night. She didn't always understand Tristan: sometimes the look in his eyes was cold, stern, a little contemptuous, and then she panicked—had she displeased him? She felt clearly that he was less attached to her than she was to him, and, secretly, this inequality caused her pain. Without him, everything would fall apart.

When she saw Tristan having lunch with another woman, she felt that something between them was breaking. She was terribly jealous. And that was as difficult for him as for her. She admired those women who remain confident, who manage to be their usual selves under all circumstances. She regarded them as having an elegance and a strength of which she felt incapable. That is why she detested them.

In the evening, they went to the theatre, and she asked

Tristan what he had done that day. He claimed he had had lunch with Nicolas. She said nothing, but she felt such strong disgust that her stomach began to complain. Her illusions were gently turning into nausea.

11

DOWNSTAIRS, the main lobby of the Royal Hotel was flooded with sunlight, and Amélie put her hand up to her face. What luck, she thought, the weather's really lovely for September! If this keeps up, we'll be able to swim.

Suddenly her expression freezes: placed next to the reception desk, she has just spotted a red suitcase, and she has the feeling that she recognises it. The thing may seem improbable, and yet I am merely narrating what happened, nothing more.

Every day for the past two months, she had seen a woman just below their apartment, in the rue de Verneuil. Apparently she lived on the street, but always in the same place, a few metres from their door. She seemed never to move away, not even a few hundred metres. She had adopted a bit of pavement and, it seemed, wouldn't have changed it for anything in the world. The particular thing about her was that she transported four enormous coloured suitcases with her. She held them closely to her as if she was afraid that someone would come and steal them from her. When she went to buy something at the baker's shop opposite, she picked them up one by one and carried them to the other side of the street. Amélie had always wondered what they might contain. Is it something vital to a wanderer's life? What do you carry with you when you don't live anywhere?

In any case, she was always dressed in the same way: so it probably wasn't clothes. She slept in the same spot and no doubt never washed. Sometimes, when she was coming home late from a party, Amélie had seen how she organised herself: she laid the suitcases down on the ground and stretched out on top of them. Without really knowing why, Amélie was intrigued by this woman. What did she do? What was her story? Sometimes she also observed her, from high up in her apartment. She was on the pavement, directly opposite. She would very much have liked to go and give her a little money, but she didn't dare do it.

One day, Amélie had gone down to make some photo-copies, and this woman had just gone into the shop, madly abandoning her suitcases in the street. She was holding a lit-tle wallet containing a few documents: bills probably found on café terraces, bits of paper picked up off the ground, pamphlets, dead leaves. As she saw that Amélie was observ-ing her, she explained to her that she was putting together a file, all she lacked were the last few items, but it was practi-cally complete.

"What sort of file?" asked Amélie.

"A file to get my name back. Because I have no name. Somebody stole it from me, you see. But the court case is under way, and I think I am going to get it back soon."

"Who stole your name from you?"

"In fact, I was born without a name. Just an initial. That's why I can't work."

Then she handed her wallet to the copy-shop boy and asked him for ten copies of her "official documents". Clear-ly she was a little mad.

Then, a few days before leaving for Deauville, Amélie had noticed she wasn't there any more. She had disappeared. But one thing disturbed her even more: she had abandoned one of her suitcases, the red one. Would she come back to fetch it? Amélie hesitated. She would very much have liked to know what was inside, but she didn't dare go and open it.

And now she was at the seaside and standing in front of

that same suitcase. Presently a woman came and picked it up. She visibly had difficulty in carrying it. Of course, it wasn't the same suitcase, but merely a red suitcase, of which thousands must exist. The woman seemed rather young. From the back, she even appeared pretty. Amélie watched her walk away and step into the lift cage; when the doors closed again, she felt a profound discomfort as if she had just lost someone who was dear to her.

"Do you remember the woman with her suitcases?" she asked Tristan later.

"The one from down below?"

"Yes. Well, she's disappeared. It's strange, don't you think?"

She wanted to explain to him about the red suitcase in the hotel lobby too, but she decided not to; if she did, she'd look like a madwoman too.

12

SHE CROSSED the lobby and, a little troubled, went out of the hotel's main door. The wind was cooler than she'd expected. She crossed the road and, once she was on the boardwalk, took off her shoes. She preferred walking barefoot on the beach. This sensation always took her back to something distant within her, something primitive or very ancient. People ought to be banned from wearing shoes on the beach, she thought.

It was low tide. The cries of a few gulls could be heard. Amélie suddenly stopped walking and closed her eyes; under her eyelids, the sun drew orange patches until a cloud, the eyelid of autumn, temporarily covered the sky; a shiver went through her and she started walking again. There was practically no-one on the beach. The majestic whiteness of the gulf had been waiting since dawn. The coloured parasols were closed. The setting seemed to be refusing to play the game. She wanted first of all to pick up a shell and bring it back to Tristan. She liked them a lot, the ones in which you could hear the sea. Then she had the idea of finding the holiday property in which she'd spent two summers with her cousins. Then she was seized by an enthusiasm that astonished herself, as if this house, which she had up till then perfectly forgotten, had suddenly become the most important place in her life.

According to her memories, it stood beside the beach, in the direction of Blonville. You could naturally recognise it by the windmill that adjoined it. Tristan is going to wake up soon, she told herself. Perhaps I should go there with him later. But she continued her walk.

As she walked, she attempted to remember. Then details came back to her memory. Like that night when she had gone out with her cousin. Their bedroom led into a small bathroom, whose window opened onto the garden. The two girls had waited until everyone in the house was asleep before escaping. She would never have done it on her own, and she remembers that she was really afraid. But her cousin was much bolder and she seemed not to fear anything. What did they do, that night? Curiously, she couldn't remember anything at all about it. Perhaps they had gone to the town centre. Near the casino? On the beach? She was incapable of remembering exactly.

A little boy was running after a plastic bag that the wind was blowing along. She looked at the sky. Would the clouds disappear? On the contrary, there seemed to be more and more of them. She put her shoes back on and continued walking. All the shops were shut. It was too early. The wind strengthened at the same moment, and a shutter that hadn't been properly closed started to bang. "It's all going wrong," she said out loud. She glanced towards the horizon to evaluate the distance she still had left to cover. She had no idea how far it was, and this road seemed a lot longer than in her memories. Perhaps the best thing would be to ask the way. She went into a café.

13

S HE PUSHED open the door and immediately had the feeling that everybody was looking at her—a feeling of discomfort overwhelmed her. She walked forward to the counter. A chubby guy was serving, and Amélie felt even more ill at ease: he probably thought that she was going to buy something from him. She didn't dare tell him that she only wanted directions.

"Do you have cigarettes, by any chance?"

He nodded yes, and she bought a packet. Then she explained to him that she was looking for a house that, as she remembered it, ought to be around here somewhere. A house with a windmill, she added.

"With a windmill? There's no windmill around here!"

"A windmill, or something that looks like one, a tower or something. I haven't been back in years, but … "

"No, I tell you," he said with a touch of impatience. "I know what I'm saying, I've lived here for thirty years. You've been misinformed!"

She wanted to persist, but a woman, who was giving her an evil look, was already approaching to find out what was going on. She said her thanks and was about to go.

Turning back, she noticed a couple in the corner of the café; and then an astonishing emotion shot through her. (He was looking right into her eyes as he held her hands, as if he was telling her all his deepest secrets; and she was looking at him with so much attention—or perhaps it was passion—and smiling mysteriously.)

Why was she disturbed by this couple, who were after all quite ordinary? In the time it took her to ask herself the question, she was already outside. Too late, impossible to go back, she should have had the reflex of sitting at a table so that she could observe them. She cast a final glance through the window, but she saw only the reflection of the beach.

She continued on the same road, then took a left turn. She spent a long time walking along all the narrow streets. But it seemed to her that the more she attempted to remember, the more her memory failed her. She now doubted the images she had considered authentic a moment before. Was she certain about the windmill? For, indeed, she had not seen anything that could have resembled a windmill. The house of her childhood remained unfound and, along with it, all those years which had left her with a vague feeling of sweetness.

14

SHE DECIDED to give up. She turned on her heel and headed for the hotel. Tristan must be dressed by now. "I ought to have left him a note, telling him that I was leaving," she told herself. She wondered if she ought to take a short cut via the beach, but continued on the road. Soon, she spotted the flags that flew over the Royal.

She passed the café a second time. Once again, the sun reappeared, and she crossed to the other pavement so as not to walk in the shade. "It's strange, the weather is really changeable."

Suddenly, far off on the beach, she thought she recognised the couple she had seen a little while before, and was seized by dizziness. She headed in their direction, and the shorter the distance that separated her from them became, the more disturbed she felt. She had the strange feeling of having known them if not forever—at least for a very long time, while in fact she knew quite well that she didn't know them at all.

They were standing facing the sea. The woman was pointing at the horizon. At that moment they were all the lovers in the world, they were the happiness of being two, the fevered and magnificently puerile hope of being just one. As she watched them, Amélie was seized by a violent feeling of melancholy. She dared not approach. Who were they? He was tall and slender and wore a dark suit. Why was he so elegant on the beach? And what about her? She had a short dress and long blonde hair. They look really beautiful together, Amélie told herself. They look happy. It was then that the bluish horizon seemed to her to be a line of no return.

She overtook them. Why did she feel so sad? She waited until she was far enough away from them to turn back for a last time. They were still there, kissing.

She was sad because it seemed to her that everything was destined to pass away, to wither, to decay. One day, they'll have to surrender, she thought. One day, they'll detest each other. Beginnings don't mean anything. Yes, beginnings lie, and everything passes away.

15

WHEN SHE ARRIVED at the hotel, she turned round for one last time: they had disappeared. A little stupidly, she wondered where they could have gone and, suddenly, her dream came back to torment her.

She imagined the couple who had just disappeared leaving eagerly for Brazil, unaware of the horrors of that destination. She found this story moving. She sees that man in the dark suit scouring the whole country to find the girl who's been taken from him, never loving her as much as when she is not there, torn away; tortured, tortured by her absence. Talking aloud to her as if she were still there.

"Tell me, will we ever really see each other again?"

His questions remained unanswered. The splendour of love. And its cruelty.

Where can she be? At the commissariat in Rio, they explain to him that this kind of kidnapping is common at the moment. Now, she is undoubtedly working in a bordello somewhere in the country. It is then that the lover begins to love her with an infinite love, now that she has gone. And Amélie sees herself, drugged in a bar at the end of the world, subjected to the unthinkable at every moment, but saved by this certainty that she is loved, torturing the loved one by her absence, saved forever …

Do you have to go away in order to be loved? She clings to Tristan, and she clearly sees that he is distancing himself, she knows that there are other women, and that if he remains with her, it is more out of compassion than love. What then? Disappear? Die? How many times has she imagined her own death? She can only succeed in feeling loved by imagining herself being missed. People will weep over her. They will miss her. And Tristan will seek her throughout the land, in despair because he has lost her. And then, in his turn, he will lose himself in conjuring up what they could have experienced together. Too late. Too late. She is gone! Remember how she smiled! And the way she had of leaning her head to one side when she was intimidated! And her eyes! And the small of her back! Too late! She had a fragile, terribly feminine voice. And all this must now be buried. You can keep trying to dig into the earth, you can break your nails, but it's too late, once and for all! She has disappeared! She belongs to the family of the angels now.

16

THE LOBBY was swarming with people. Several police officers were talking to the hotel owner. Amélie wondered what was happening. She questioned the person next to her. "I don't know," she said with a conspiratorial smile. There was nothing much to be seen, if you don't count the chaos of a spontaneous gathering. Everyone was trying to make themselves taller so as to see over all the heads. Nobody knew exactly what they were hoping to find out, but there was a crowd there, and that must guarantee something extraordinary, since it is so unusual these days to see people taking an interest in one another, except through voyeurism.

Amélie pushed her way through the crowd and tried to take the lift, but one of the policemen barred her way. "Use the stairs," he ordered her tartly. Then, having considered her, he added more courteously: "The lift's not working."

So she took the stairs. At the second floor, she speeded up, seized by a stupid intuition. What if Tristan had something to do with this crowd? A shiver ran through her. She thought of Brazil, of the lovers who never see each other again, and she started running up the stairs.

She reached the door, opened it, and entered the room. The window was still open, the curtains ballooning slightly. "Tristan?"

No reply. He wasn't in the bed any more. She spun around as if, on one last inspection, she hoped to fall upon him. "Where is he?" she asked out loud. His things weren't there any more. Suddenly she had the atrocious feeling that she had always known. Events were merely confirming her successive intuitions. She panicked. She realised that this was the end.

She left the room as she had entered it, running, and left the door open. She leaned out over the void, over the lift cage, but she saw nothing. Then she hurtled, hurtled down the stairs to reception. She held on to the banister. Her feet wanted to trip each other up. She felt as if she were missing a step. Quickly. Where is he? Already, she felt violent spasms in her belly. The end, she told herself once again. Isn't this what she's been silently preparing for since the beginning, as if nothing else could come to pass but her own end?

There were slightly fewer people around. She looked around for someone who could provide her with information. Reception. No. Too many people. And what would she say to them? Quickly. Turn round. There, a police officer who's wandered off.

"Excuse me."

"Are you looking for something?"

"What's happening?"

"Nothing, nothing, don't get upset," he told her with a smile that was intended to be reassuring. "There's been a little accident."

"I'm looking for my fiancé!"

The police officer's expression became more serious, only increasing Amélie's panic.

"You've lost sight of him?"

"He's not in the room any more!"

"Perhaps he's gone out for a walk," he ventured.

She took a step backwards. She realised that she was ridiculous. It's that story about lovers, she thought.

She thanked him in a voice that was practically inaudible and decided to go back up and wait in the room. As she headed for the stairs, she noticed a woman on the ground, looking as if she'd fainted, or was perhaps dead, and a crowd around her.

Yes, he's probably gone out for a walk. He saw that I wasn't there any more and told himself he'd find me on the beach. In any event, it can only be that.

The door was closed now. The wind, the open window. She entered the room.

Tristan was standing by the bed, a towel around his waist. It was clear that he had just come out of the shower.

She would have liked to throw herself into his arms, but she didn't dare.

"You're here?" she said.

"Well, yes! You look astonished … Is something wrong?"

She approached him.

"I thought I wasn't going to see you again … "

He began to laugh.

"What on earth are you talking about?"

17

WHAT SHE IS TALKING about: "The dead remains of illusions, the solitary walks, all the deserts of our dual solitude, the promises of circumstances, depravity, drought, the insolent barrier of numbers, paragraphs, the excess of indecisions, secret tyrannies, the attraction of death, all the underground attacks, wars and insurrections; the appeal, the fascination of the infinite, the fear of death, the Royal, the beach, the sand, the beach's splendid curve, the life that unfolds without us and which will abandon us there, in the shadow of childish hopes, bottom-of-the-range tragedies, voiceless cries, starless skies, purposeless torments; toads, shrews and seals, chance, the bookshop, the windmill, pedestrian crossings, debauchery, the temptation to scatter, the anxieties, the bitten nails, the burning sensations in the stomach, and the sensation of not being able to do anything about them; the dizziness, the distance, the silence, the fear of losing oneself, of never seeing each other again, the Brazilian taxi at the kerb, the harshness and the insults, the lessening, the delight of sleep—the delight of death."

18

TRISTAN WAS still in his office. He had planned to come and fetch Amélie at the end of school and leave directly for Deauville. He was meant to have lunch with Nicolas, but no longer wanted to.

For a few weeks now, Nicolas had been in love, and other people's happiness has something indecent about it, even when you know that it is temporary and founded on illusions that life will rapidly take care of dispelling. Tristan wanted to give his secretary a call and ask her to cancel it, but in the end he didn't.

He stayed another two hours in his office, doing nothing. He considered his life as a whole and could not get rid of the disgust he had been feeling for several days. What remained of his former passionate enthusiasms? Practically nothing. He had died away. What's more, everything around him seemed dramatically extinct. No more madness. No more enthusiasm. Nothing.

Standing at his window, he is now looking at the building opposite, and through a play of light, his face appears on the windowpane. Is it not the face of a weak man? Then his brows knit in a frown. When he was an adolescent, he sincerely believed that a special destiny awaited him. He felt superior to the others. Around him, people submitted. At that time he had a sombre face, incapable of compromise—sombre and proud. Today, he is sometimes so afraid of being alone that he would prefer to spend time with someone insignificant than with himself.

Superior beings are loners, thinks Tristan. He knows very well, he has not been up to the mark of the person he would have liked to be. He has spoiled the start of his life with small ambitions, small demands, small pleasures. He would have liked it to be heroic, his life. Sublime. He would have liked to be capable of great passions, to immolate himself for the sake of ridiculous things, and for everything around him to be splendid. He would have liked to know how to sacrifice everything for an absolute, whatever it might be. To be generous, noble, hard. Not to fall into considerations of half-measures, not to abandon himself to mediocrity. But things are obvious now: he belongs to the race of the half-hearted. The only thing he will have left in the world is the fact that he sometimes wept. And he does so again.

Tristan looks around him: his office, his chair, his telephone, his files; and he feels a tiredness he can't explain. It's true, he had thought he felt within himself all the axioms of a sublime destiny. He was going to become a great man, and his torments would inevitably be in proportion to that promise made to the future—excessive. Today, it is above all their smallness, the smallness of his torments, which sadden him. Finally, he has become a vulgar being whose internal conflicts look more like bourgeois whims. The worst aspect of his behaviour is this facility with which he finds justifications and extenuating circumstances for himself. Back then, he was in revolt against himself, he led permanent revolutions—and don't you measure the power of an individual by the sum of his disagreements with himself? And then, suddenly, his illusions lost their virulence and modestly made their way towards indifference, towards disgust, towards mediocrity.

19

THEN TRISTAN'S SECRETARY comes into the office and informs him that Nicolas has just cancelled lunch.

Tristan looks at her without surprise. He is well aware why Nicolas reproaches him.

In love? He realises that he envies him. Love is without doubt the only interesting thing in the world. As an adolescent, OK. But now? He no longer believes in it, it is no longer possible.

They met several years ago. Today, their friendship is threatened by a thousand small things, those compromises, those misunderstandings you lumber yourself with as you get older. There was Amélie first of all. Women are the cancer of friendship. "You don't love her! So why set up home with her?" he had asked him at the time. Tristan hadn't dared answer that it was through weakness, to compensate for the sufferings he made her endure. "I love her, that's all," he had simply said. And so as not to be suspected of contradictions, Tristan had never talked to him about his infidelities.

Nicolas had a romantic vision of love, a vision that was pure but often grotesque. He invested everything with a sort of absolute and could not understand that someone might hesitate, torture himself with indecision, go back on his choices.

Three years earlier, he had fallen in love with a woman he had followed to New York. He had abandoned everything for her and could not conceive that anyone could do otherwise. In New York, according to what he had been told, they had lived in a dirty little hotel in the middle of junkies and whores. For six months, they had stayed in this hole, in the middle of the worst sorts of ugliness, permeable to the obscenity of the world, to its mud-spattered voracity. In the end, the girl dumped him and he went back to France.

Somewhat by chance, he allowed himself to be carried away by journalism, for which he had absolutely no aptitude, apart from a taste for laziness and a certain insincerity. However, he practically never worked. "Nicolas is working" was a phrase that was sufficiently improbable to have become funny as a result. More precisely, he had this peculiarity, that he worked no more than two weeks per year, but when he was working, everybody had to know it: he was the sort to call you simply to warn you that, if by chance you were hoping to see him within the next two weeks, it really wasn't possible, his diary was as full as the theatre staging the play he secretly dreamed of writing.

20

SO THE MAN who secretly dreamed of writing had cancelled their meeting. Yes, Tristan knew why he was reproaching him. He was reproaching him for that terrible laugh he had let out, a week before, and that way of looking at his Aurore, the one who inspired mad love and fits of anger! Had he really attempted to seduce her right under Nicolas's nose? I believe rather that Tristan had simply wanted to threaten him, to threaten this love which he took for an absolute, and to play of course, always to play. But why did he have this need to wreck everything around him? It was a normal party. Amélie hadn't come; she'd chosen to go to bed early instead. It was the first time he'd met Aurore. From a distance, first. She was in conversation with several people. Tristan found her beautiful. However she wasn't a patch on those exceptional women, the mere sight of whom transports you into indecent reveries, and it wasn't difficult to make out a few flaws on her face, but—was it that insistence in the eyes or the mystery of a woman who, suddenly, belongs to someone?—Tristan had felt something like the silent conspiracy of destiny between them.

He approached her a little later in the evening. It was then that he caught himself lightly seducing her. The distant but concentrated gaze, the rather offhand manner, charming but disinterested, a little disdainful, sure of himself, the whole panoply of cut-price seduction, but she seemed amused by the game.

"Do you write too?" she asked him at one point.

Tristan let out an odious laugh.

"Why 'too'?"

Often, Nicolas did not consider it useful to make the distinction between "being a writer" and "hoping one day to become one". In this way he passed for someone he wasn't, and he was right since women were not insensible to it. (What's more, in a general way, they only like men who vaguely resemble a simplistic and preconceived image of perfection, an image available in the smallest of brains. But as the inevitable masculine decline progresses, discovering that the chosen one diverges dramatically from this initial projection, they begin to buy him jackets to give him the elegance he lacks; still under the cover of generosity, they give him the perfume they smelled the previous evening on a more virile figure, next they encourage him to play sport so that he can approximate this figure they would like to embrace, and the dressing up continues until the day they decide it would be amazingly chic to go out with an "artist", and, that's how our martyred little man, in addition to the jackets and the perfume, is set to work, his soul in distress.)

So Nicolas had become a writer, perhaps even one of the most promising of his generation, with the small caveat that he had never written anything. What's more, why did he dream of writing? The recognition? To make her falsely in love with him? Everywhere you see suffering people, capable of anything for these poor panaceas. Each morning, they repeat the same prayer, imploring the person they would like to be to please happen, they talk loudly—but secretly, they detest themselves.

"Do I write 'too'?" Tristan repeated amicably. This very evening I am going to save my best friend from the absurdity of a love affair, and into the bargain, save a woman from the absurdity of my best friend. I am capable of all this spinelessness. So why would I write 'too'?

You couldn't bear that laugh and that bottom-of-the-range seduction. And in your eyes, I can already make out kilometres of reproach, and, barely escaping from a closed mouth, admissions of defeat. Yes, I can even make out what you're saying, Nicolas. You are reproaching me for being destructive, for destroying everything that is created without me. To make the case against me even worse, you refer to the feelings you have for her. You tell yourself that I am one of those who, sensing that they're falling, prefer not to fall alone. One of those who constantly seek to diminish themselves, as if they were deprived of love once and for all. I am not trying to corrupt your hopes mate, life will take care of that very efficiently, I am just trying to save mine, to discover a new way to be free.

I know a mad old woman who, knowing that her house could collapse at any moment, has been waiting for years in the cold for the thing to happen, cursing the fact that it hasn't happened yet. I am that mad old woman, Nicolas. I am waiting for the collapse, I am calling it to me, to come and deliver me from the waiting. And the sooner the better. Perhaps one day you will also know this intense pleasure you can feel in sacrificing everything, in using every possibility of salvation as a target, and knocking it down, doing it in, and beginning again until you can't any more, bang! and turning over the corpse with a kick of your boot. Or conversely, saving it: bending over someone, diverting him from his former desires and imposing new ones on him, more harmful ones, so that he dies of them.

21

HE GOT UP and left his office. In barely two hours' time, he would go and fetch Amélie when her school came out and they would leave lovingly for Deauville. He had no desire to work. He decided to walk, to stroll through the streets at random. Curiously, the thought came to him of going to the Polish Bookshop. He'd never actually been inside.

He entered as though it were a temple. He looked around him. Books were laid on a table, others lined up on shelves; although Polish, it was a completely ordinary bookshop. Suddenly, one of the sales girls happened to see him and had this strange reaction.

"So, I see, you're interested in poetry then?"

Tristan was a little surprised. He didn't know what to reply. He shrugged his shoulders vaguely. One way of saying yes, but nothing more.

"Oh, really? I had the feeling you bought poetry every time. I thought, but perhaps … "

"Me?"

"Perhaps I'm mistaken, I … "

"No, I don't think so. Let it be me."

"I must have the wrong person. It can't be you after all … "

"No … It's somebody else."

He gave her an awkward smile, thanked her and left the bookshop.

As he walked, he thought again of his meeting with Amélie. It was still to this region of his memory that he came to draw his affection. He thought back to that way she'd had of crossing the pedestrian crossing. He had the impression that he knew perfectly the secrets of her games, the intimacy of her mad moments. Sometimes, I watch you from afar, my radiant one! I watch you and I can make out what is happening inside your head. That mask you hung up in the sitting room, the one you brought back from Africa, once I caught you talking to it out loud, you were asking it if it wasn't too cold, like that, a mask, then you went and closed the sitting room window. A few days later, I saw that you had bought a CD of African music, I know because I know you perfectly, I know that sometimes you put it on so that it doesn't feel too homesick, a mask! Your sweet madness, it is made for me, darling, that of your loneliness, when you think that nobody can see you and you start dancing, beautiful one, like that, that's what I love in you, and in a little while we shall be in Deauville!

Then, as planned, he goes to the jeweller's shop that stands next to his apartment. There are no customers inside. He buys a ring. He takes the most beautiful one in the shop. Will she like it?

Then he gets his things ready for leaving. He thinks of what's going to happen there, and a shiver passes through him. Then he gets his car and drives to Amélie's school. He parks just in front of the entrance, and just as he switches off the engine, the bell rings. A few minutes later, Amélie appears on the forecourt, wearing a summer dress. She waves to him and approaches the car.

"Are we going straight there?" she asks excitedly.

"Unless you need to call in at the apartment."

"Er ... Have you got my bag?"

"It's in the back."

"Then we can go!"

A little later, he pulls over; she wants to buy some

cigarettes. Tristan takes advantage of this to ask her to post an envelope. He looks for it in his things and hands it to her. "What is it?" He says something inaudible and she doesn't persist. She looks at it: it resembles a business letter. She shrugs her shoulders and gets out of the car.

While he waits, the idea comes to him that he could leave, suddenly drive off and leave. She comes back a moment later, the cigarettes in her hand. It's then that Tristan tells himself that she could quite well have got into another car and continued her life elsewhere. She could have been an anonymous woman buying a packet of cigarettes, a woman who would never have entered his life. In fact, everything could quite well not have happened.

Why her and not another? he asks himself once again.

She opens the door, sits down beside him and pulls a face. "That's it, we can go!" Suddenly, Tristan feels a fierce anguish. He is already starting to feel regret. Perhaps it wasn't a good idea after all, Deauville, the ring. All this.

22

YOU'RE HERE?
Tristan looks at her, a little surprised. A towel around his waist. She looks panicky.

"Well, yes! You look astonished ... Is something wrong?"

She approaches him. She would like to take him in her arms. She was afraid.

"I thought I wouldn't see you again ... "

He starts to laugh.

"What are you on about?"

Suddenly, she regrets having said it.

"Are you ready?"

A little while ago, they walked to the port. Now, I can see them in a restaurant in the town centre, a restaurant reputed for its fish. The hotel reception guaranteed that it was one of the best in town. Tristan has taken with him the ring he bought the previous evening in Paris.

"Do you remember the girl with her suitcases?"Amélie asks him.

"The one from down below?"

"Yes. Well, she's disappeared. It's strange, isn't it?"

Tristan is scarcely listening to her. Married, we'll be as lively as these dead fish, he tells himself suddenly. When you think about it: what's more fucking stupid than all the things that live in the sea? No anguish for them. No anxiety. Wisdom is sea-based. But, in the end, isn't it in his inner torments that man finds his dignity? The majority of people resemble fish. Digestive irony.

Amélie is talking to him about a vague plan.

"Just before, when I was walking, I saw a guest house. It was a little house with Virginia creeper … "

"You'd have preferred sleeping in a guest house?"

"No, but I told myself I would so have liked to live with you in that kind of place. You see, leave Paris and open a guest house, like that. It can't demand a lot of work, a guest house. Anyway, when I say 'a' guest house I mean several. So that we could make a living. No? The interesting bit must be that you get to meet different people every day."

"Tourists?"

"Not just tourists … Wouldn't you like it, living like that at the seaside? Not living in Paris any more … "

Tristan is breathing hard. Alone here, with her, the morning with her, the evening with her. He will tell her that she is the scent of the lilac and the sound of the rain in the garden …

After lunch, they decide to go on the beach. At one point, Amélie spots a woman stretched out in the middle of the road. Several people are around her now. A car has gone into a street-lamp, probably while trying to avoid her. Amélie stops for a moment; it's the second person she's seen on the ground today. The one who's been run over is blonde; you'd think it was a scene from a film.

They settle themselves under an orange parasol. Tristan reads while Amélie seems to sleep. From time to time, she raises herself up on her elbows and looks at the horizon, brows furrowed. "Don't you want to swim?" Her stomach seems to be faring much better. Or you'd think so. "No, not now, but you go."

A few women pass by in swimming costumes; Tristan puts down his book. It is the insistent torture of the world come back to try him. The procession of temptation. As far back as he can remember, he has always been captivated by women's bodies, he has always been able to detect some mystery there, some obsession. Sometimes, this horrible thought comes into his mind: how much would he have given never to have met her?

And as if she could read his thoughts, Amélie gives him a nasty look, then gets up without a word. He knows that she is not happy. He ought to catch up with her, tell her that ... But he does nothing. He closes his eyes.

23

HE HAS BROUGHT the ring, in a box hidden in his bag. He doesn't know yet when he will give it to her. He can already imagine her joy. Amélie has a particular relationship with the objects that are dear to her, a relationship that isn't far from obscurantism. One day, Tristan gave her a white orchid. First of all Amélie put it in the sitting room, then changed its place a dozen times. According to her, there was more sun in the bedroom, but less noise in the kitchen: how was she to choose? She treated it like a human being. All at once, she felt guilty at not giving it enough attention. She sprayed water on its leaves with the clumsiness of a young mother.

In her former studio flat, when she lived alone, her attention to things was even more mysterious. The African mask for example. Likewise with her soft toys, which had always occupied the end of her bed. How was she to explain to them that she wanted to get rid of them without annoying them? She took them away one by one. But there again: how could she choose? What was she to do not to set them against each other? Amélie was convinced that this was a real problem. She must explain to them calmly; they would understand, at least it was to be hoped so.

I have already talked about another of her fancies, this impression that she was being permanently watched. When it wasn't by her mother, it seemed to her that another gaze was passing through all these objects. Or that, behind the walls, certain boys of her own age, those she had been in love with as a child, were permanently spying on her and judging her. So she must be faithful, without respite, to the image she wanted to portray. Any relaxation became inconceivable. This is how she had visualised the demands one can have upon oneself. And her culpability in relation to the world.

What did she feel guilty of? Her mother had never told her how she was born, but she had clearly understood that her father was not the kind of man to settle down with a family. After his departure for Germany, he had travelled a lot, always, no doubt, to flee from some point of anchorage or other. But he came back to France regularly and dropped by to see Amélie. He too felt a certain culpability, to the extent that he had not always been very present as a father. And as if to justify himself, he had attempted several times to explain to her why he had left. Amélie absorbed the lesson: if he had married her mother, it was solely because she had been pregnant, and if her mother had become depressive, it was because she had lost her husband. Thus, in an indirect way, she had become the cause of her mother's distress.

24

FROM THAT MOMENT on, there was no end to her desire to stop existing. As a little girl, she practically never spoke, so she was considered to be unhealthily timid. But her unconscious will to disappear took a more worrying form during her adolescence: she practically stopped eating. Her mother took a while to realise that her daughter was anorexic.

Amélie looked at herself in the mirror: she found real consolation in coming closer, little by little, to non-existence; soon, she would no longer be. The sensation of emptiness inside merged perfectly, in her mind, with the notion of purity, even chastity: eating was sullying herself with the outside world, sleeping with all the taints of others. Sometimes she had attacks of dizziness, fainting fits, moments when she lost control, and that was delicious.

Her mother could not understand her obstinacy and at first took no interest in it, before becoming excessively worried about it. She had just found the argument for her vengeance. Indeed, the doctor was already talking about hospitalisation. And if one had to find someone responsible in this matter, it was without any doubt this absent father. Through her daughter, the mother was going to be able to detain her fugitive husband and lock him up in the meanest of prisons, that of guilt. She was going to fulfil herself by means of her daughter: what she hadn't done, her daughter was going to do.

Amélie fell ill and temporarily stopped studying. But she still refused to feed herself. She did not know exactly what she was seeking in acting this way; what's more, was she seeking something precise? She found herself faced with a fact: she was not hungry, and this lack had become an element of her identity.

Sometimes, in the evenings, she would write letters in which she wept for her progressive demise; never had she attained such strong sensations. It was in this period that she acquired the habit of imagining her death. She did it often in her bed. She was so sad then that she could get to sleep. Her death had become the sleep ritual. She cried as though her heart would break to see herself dead.

She was taken into hospital one December. Her father came back to Paris to see her. He asked to stay alone with her. He took her hand. He talked to her in a loud voice, asked her to fight and to stay among them. Amélie kept her eyes closed, she listened attentively to everything he was telling her, but made as if she couldn't hear. She was at last that dead woman over whom people were weeping. Well! Was it enough not to eat to bring an absent father back to you?

25

TRISTAN HAD told her in an innocent voice that he had had lunch with Nicolas, whereas she had seen him with a girl in a restaurant, near the Odéon. If he wasn't telling her the truth, it was because it was in his interest to hide it. Now, why would it be in his interest to hide this lunch if it did not reveal anything else? The worst thing for her was the assurance with which he had lied to her. How, from now on, could she know if he was telling the truth or lying?

"With Nicolas?"

"Yes we went to the Magnolia."

Amélie hadn't dared tell him that she had seen him with someone else. She was too afraid of unleashing a fatal argument. Not giving herself the right to explanations, she must confine herself to permanent suspicion—which, in many respects, is a crueller punishment.

That evening, they went to the theatre. She didn't hear a single word of the play. What's more, today, she can't even remember the name of that play. Her entire being was suffused with doubt. She ought to resent him, go away, leave him perhaps, but instead of that, and to the contempt of her own dignity, she found herself beside him again, in a theatre auditorium, as if nothing was amiss. And this violence, which she ought to have expressed against him, she redirected against herself: she resented herself for not having the courage to reproach him for his lies, she considered herself weak, she was everything she didn't like—and then she felt a profound disgust with herself. She had a terrible stomach-ache. She got up and left the auditorium.

An hour later, Tristan was at her bedside, like her father

before, and was asking her why she had got up, why she had left without warning him; she merely replied that she had a stomach-ache. This annihilation of herself, this painful disappearance she had begun in her childhood, she was at last going to be able to carry through to its end. In the end, she could only reign when she was dying.

26

THIS MORNING, Amélie goes on, I went for a walk while you were sleeping and I tried to find the house my aunt rented for two summers, but I didn't find it ...

Tristan looks at her as she gets changed. He is stretched out on the bed, his head upside down, and he is admiring her. Her long legs, the softness of her skin, the bare area of her shoulder. Signs of eternity.

He thinks again about what she was saying just now about the guest house. Would he like to live here with her, distance himself from the world? He strangely loves Paris, this peculiar energy that lets you hope, each day, that perhaps something new is going to happen. A deliverance? He senses that he needs this bustle around him, as others need alcohol to intoxicate themselves.

A little while ago, when the sun was less in evidence, they took the car and drove for a time: Tristan wanted to see the cliffs to the west of Deauville. He has always liked deserted cliffs. He has always felt a sensation of dizziness in looking at the sea and, at the same time, a sort of attraction, an unadmitted desire to jump—which is the same thing in the end, in so far as jumping would be a way of succumbing to this dizziness. They walked on the path that ran along the coast, then Amélie wanted to go back. Tristan stayed there alone for a while, facing that deserted sea, with the wind blowing in the trees behind him. He thought of those paintings of the North, where you see a solitary man standing facing the infinity of the sea. Amélie was waiting for him in the car. He was well aware that staying in this way, the spectacle of nature would quickly turn to introspection, and he found that disagreeable. He felt old. Twenty-nine. For him, that was old already, already the age of compromises. If it is permitted to consider life as a slow process of demolition, he feels that what he cared most about is now behind him. Being old has no age. Then he turns away from the horizon, from the sun, comes back to the car, and drives off.

Now, like a mysterious echo to his own reflection, he is stretched out on the double bed, he is looking at her, her long legs, the softness of her skin, the promises of her tenderness, and Amélie, as she gets changed, tells him that this morning, while he was sleeping, she attempted to find her childhood house, but that she didn't find it.

"It's disappeared," she adds, pulling a childish face.

27

SHE TELLS herself that life is beautiful, not in opposition to its ugliness, but beyond, for it is constructed like a novel, with a hidden meaning: it is not enough to turn the pages, but to allow yourself to be convinced by the mechanism of the words, the insistent mechanism of the words that repeats itself, and repeats itself insidiously to gain access to the hidden meaning.

When they come out of the restaurant, Amélie doesn't want to go back right away, she would like to go for a walk. It is quite mild. She holds onto his arm. They walk past the casino, whose front is hypocritically white. Tristan has always liked gambling, unlike Amélie who considers it vulgar and unhealthy. He doesn't suggest to her that they go in.

They are now sitting on the terrace of the Bar du Soleil, facing the sea. There are a lot of people there. "It's Saturday night," Amélie diagnoses. They settle themselves at a table, don't say anything. Next to them is a group which is making a lot of noise, and somewhere up above floats a fat reddish moon.

"It makes you want to go for a swim," says Amélie.

Among them, Tristan notices a guy of about twenty, brown and sipping a cocktail. He says something that Tristan can't hear, and the two rather beautiful girls who are sitting next to him start laughing. Without really knowing why, Tristan then feels a very strong sort of attraction towards him, an irrefutable desire to talk to him.

"What's the matter?" Amélie asks him.

Tristan discreetly shows her his neighbour and tells her that he has the feeling he has seen him before, at the same time knowing that it isn't this impression that is disturbing him, but something of a different order, something more subtle.

"It's funny, this morning I came across a couple too, and I had the same feeling. That I'd seen them before."

The truth is that he would pay dearly to be in his place. Handsome, young, sitting between two beautiful girls whom he makes laugh. The whole night before them. Life too. This sight then gives a more concrete dimension to his nostalgia. Now he is going to get married. Everyone in his turn. He will also have to agree to die one day.

He still hasn't given her the ring. He tries to imagine their wedding.

Everyone will meet up near Chartres, in Amélie's grandmother's house. After the celebration, they'll go into the garden. The weather's fine, despite a rather strong wind: several times, Amélie's mother's hat nearly flies off.

It's the first time Tristan has met Amélie's father, which gives this day a slightly surrealistic turn. So, you're marrying my daughter? How charming! One by one, the guests come up to congratulate them. It's at this moment that Tristan realises that the majority of the people who are there leave him completely indifferent. He observes them and feels a stranger to them. Worse: he feels a stranger at his own wedding.

Why this feeling? And yet he invited all the people who matter to him. What's more, this is the first time that he has brought them together and curiously, he has a diffuse feeling of solitude.

But his malaise reveals a more extensive feeling of disorientation, the giddiness of shrinking. I have already explained that Tristan lived in the fantasy of keeping himself in a world where everything would remain eternally possible. He will have put up a struggle right to the end. And what is the giddiness of shrinking, if not the odious realisation that the different possibilities are being exhausted one by one, that life is becoming specialised and confining itself to playing for ever-smaller stakes? We live in the world of speciality. We have our neighbourhoods, our friends, our apartments, our pasts, our wives, and all of this is ridiculously minuscule.

During the religious ceremony, the priest will talk about the Second Coming.

What is the Second Coming?

I think of the first Christians, to whom it was promised that salvation would come imminently, and that they would see it with their own eyes. They grew old waiting, but nothing came to pass. They died one after the other, and nothing happened. Had they been lied to?

How can you not see that as a denial of their Saviour? Unless it was a postponement, a postponement of salvation. Or perhaps it was better than a simple postponement: a revelation, a revelation on the very nature of that salvation, which is never entire, never complete, always in the process of becoming.

If salvation is always the process of becoming, the first possibility consists of believing that it must be situated at the end of where you are, and that it is enough to continue on your way to find it. As if there existed an elsewhere that conforms better to our hopes, and that this elsewhere were precisely the elsewhere towards which we were heading each day.

That's the myth of the Second Coming. The Second Coming is the only way the first Christians found of not seeing the chaos of the world as a denial of the existence of God: perfection is located precisely where one is not.

It's a given of psychological structure: I want everything I don't yet possess, I want this elsewhere that escapes me and which is the only thing enabling me to go on hoping.

The Second Coming is the inability to give up.

By getting married, however, he will promise himself that he will give up, that is to say he will abandon the hope of salvation. All at once he will find himself facing his own chaos and will be overcome by the giddiness of shrinking: henceforth, his life will be pretty much the prolongation of what it is today. He will live with Amélie. No doubt they'll have children. Et cetera.

"What are you thinking about?"

Amélie gives him a worried smile.

"Uh? Nothing."

Once again, he hears the distant sound of music, the sound of a celebration this time. By the time it reaches him it is uncertain, unreal, diffuse, and as if filtered by a dream he's been having for a long time. Then, as if his memory constituted a more comfortable refuge, Tristan rediscovers the cold sensation of Sunday evenings when, as an adolescent, he returned to the boarding school that bore all the hallmarks of a prison. Outside was life, the excitement of bodies that meet and exchange their warmth.

Once they have finished drinking, Amélie suggests to him that they go and have a swim. They approach the water to make sure it isn't too cold. The moon is still lighting up the waves.

"Told you, you can't see anything. That's what I love about swimming at night. You imagine what's underneath … "

Tristan then looks at the deserted beach. The darkness has covered the horizon again and you can effectively see nothing, except that twin moon in the water. He thinks of the beaches of Brittany where he spent all his childhood.

What has he come to look for here, in Normandy? If you can belong to a place, it's to that one, Brittany, that he belongs. He closes his eyes and, beneath his eyelids, he sees the Breton sea, a little wild, containing the shouts of children, the sun, the sound of motor boats, the wind in the billowing sails, the delicious bustle of holidays—all his life at high tide. Today, abandoned by the summer season, these beaches are deserted, but next summer they will rediscover their joys. All the next summers, the beaches will relive summers without him. And it will be the same summer indefinitely. The infinite doesn't care about him. When he has disappeared and nothing remains of him, you'll still be able to hear on these beaches the same shouts of children, the same sound of motor boats, the same wind in the billowing sails, the same delicious bustle of the summer holidays. Then Tristan clenches his fists. In the end, nothing happens, but the years flow across this kingdom of childhood, full of holes. You scarcely close your eyes, and you realise with astonishment that you already have a history, already have regrets, and wounds too.

28

AMÉLIE FEELS the water is too cold. She goes to take his hand and notices that his fist is clenched.

"Is something wrong?"

He is breathing hard, but he doesn't answer. Then she lowers her eyes and tries to understand what is happening. Has she said something she shouldn't have? She is seized by a terrible doubt. Why doesn't he answer her? And why does he still have this distant, sometimes black look in his eyes?

Amélie lets go of his hand, waits a moment to give him time to react then, despairing of his silence, turns on her heel and walks back up to the hotel, hoping that he will catch up with her, that he will contradict her, that he will explain to her, but he remains motionless, beside the water, without a word.

He comes slowly back to consciousness. Why is he acting like this? It gives the impression that he's trying deliberately to hurt her, to take revenge on her. He goes forward a few steps; his shoes are now in the water, but he doesn't react; he feels a sort of sensual pleasure at this idea. He considers the pointless stupidity of everything. What would he have wanted for his life? He no longer really knows.

He turns round and is standing in front of the hotel. Once again, the thought comes to him that he could leave. Now. Once and for all. He pants. It's strange, having the feeling that you've passed yourself by.

Then, with difficulty, he walks back up to the hotel. Amélie must be in the room. He's going to have to apologise. Console her. But isn't that the role he's always given himself?

The lobby is deserted. How he would love to be free! But

freedom is only possible for a time. He climbs the stairs. Amélie has stolen his freedom from him. He now understands that phrase that he often repeated to himself at the beginning: "She entered my life like a thief."

Sometimes, Tristan tells himself that he would like to abandon everything, in one fell swoop. He would go off and travel on his own, somewhere in the world—Brazil perhaps. Or maybe he would rediscover his childhood home, in Brittany. What would he do then? He would write no doubt. For, of course, like those who do not know how to live, he comes to be tempted by the demons of writing. People often say that it takes more courage to leave than to come back. That's forgetting that the return is also a journey, and that it demands as much courage as the outward leg, at least that's the implication.

On the third floor, he pushes open the door like a man sentenced to death. Amélie isn't there, not in the bed, or in the bathroom. Where is she? He spins round, as if he was hoping to spot her on a final inspection. She has disappeared. Suddenly, he has the impression that he has always known. He leaves the room. She is capable of anything in distress, he tells himself. A frisson of horror runs through him, and he takes it for a frisson of love.

29

HE GOES AS FAR as the stairwell, leans over the void, but sees nothing. What can he do? Where should he go and look for her? He is overcome by an irresistible panic, like that evening in the theatre. But at the same moment, he hears a sound coming from their room, whose door is still open. He retraces his steps, crosses the corridor and, from a distance, spots Amélie standing with her back to him, right in the middle of the room; doubtless she was on the terrace. He smiles inside himself, as if to mask his monstrous disappointment.

He thought that she had gone.

What next? Go back in, console her, explain himself, give her the ring? Terrible disgust. He takes a step back, but already she has spotted him. So he walks in silently. Behind him, a strange precaution, he locks the door, then goes directly into the bathroom so as not to meet her gaze. He searches for his words. Suddenly, he encounters his own face in the mirror and, once again, detects in it a fierce appetite for destruction.

Amélie is now behind him.

"I would like you to explain to me," she says in a barely audible voice. "I don't understand any more ... "

He turns round. He doesn't even want to give her an explanation. She can't bear his silence any more, so she leaves the bathroom and goes and sits down on the bed. He follows her after a slight delay, then stands in front of her. She looks at him like a child expecting to be released. The sky is heavy.

"Do you want to play dead?" he asks her with a

solemnity that frightens her.

"What?"

She had told him how she played this game, in her childhood. With her cousin. And then alone, sometimes.

"Stand up."

Hesitantly, she stands up. She knows that at the moment he tells her to fall she will fall like a dead woman; then he will come to bring her back to life and, beyond the game, this game which we have all played in our childhood, beyond the game, I don't know, a resurrection, a hope …

She stands there, her eyes lowered. She awaits the sentence.

"Turn round."

She turns round silently. At the same moment, a cloud moves, or something else changes in the sky, and the moon reappears. It lights up Amélie from the front and gives her face a pallid hue. Tristan orders her to walk towards the window. She does so faithfully, one step in front of the other, like an automaton. And suddenly; "Fall!"

So she lets herself fall to the ground as if she were really dead. Tristan is astonished to see this body respond to his smallest command; he derives a perverse pleasure from it. As it touched the floor there was a muffled sound, probably the head, but Amélie remained impassive, perfect for this role which she has rehearsed all her life, in silence.

She is now on the ground, inert.

How long could he leave her like this? Soon, she will wonder if he is really planning to come and release her, for she knows the game: she can't get up until he comes to free her. Of course, the moment he calls her, the moment he shakes her, she won't move, so that he too begins to doubt, surreptitiously to mingle the categories of false and true.

For the moment he stays there, victorious before his

victory; he contemplates her with satisfaction. He takes a step in her direction. Then another. He would like to touch the miracle of the infinite. He remembers that just now, when he entered the room and he hadn't seen her, he was run through by a frisson of horror that he took for a frisson of love. Had she gone?

He bends down, passes a hand across her face to feel her breathing. Nothing, not one breath. She plays the game admirably, she doesn't breathe when he approaches; he draws back to see if her ribs rise: apparently not. How does she manage to hold it for so long?

"Amélie!" Still no response. He shakes her a little harder. Once again, he passes his hand in front of her mouth. He looks at her, and a powerful emotion overcomes him. "Too late, it is over." She has gone! Remember how she smiled! And the way she had of leaning her head to one side when she was intimidated! And her eyes! And the small of her back! Too late! She had a fragile, terribly feminine voice. All of this must be buried now. You can keep trying to dig into this earth, you can break your nails, it's too late, once and for all! She is gone! She now belongs to the family of the angels. Ah! The thing you've been waiting for for a long time has at last come true. She will know no more of those detestable mornings when it is cold, those cruel mornings when you realise that once again the day has broken, and that we must attempt to live. She will never again be alone. And you, free at last, drunk and consoled by a real grief, a grief over which you can lament! You become aware that you never love her as much as when she is absent, and your eyes even fill with tears.

Then, prince, you bend and kiss her to release her from sleep, she opens her eyes, and is beautiful, and once again you detest her for existing: a modern fairytale.

30

AFTER THAT things move quickly. You spent the late evening close to each other. Playing dead: first worry the other person with your own death, then open your eyes and get rid of the past. You perhaps made love. It's difficult to say. Then it was time to go to bed.

But, this evening, you can't find sleep. You reflect, unless it's a dream. She is beside you, and you think back to the delight of her absence. Her body is just there, her presence is painful to you. You hear a light snore. You have never been able to leave her, and yet since the beginning you've known that's all you're waiting for. You've slept with other women, you've dragged her through the mud, you've sought to destroy her little by little so that she goes away, but she is still there, beside you, and she snores lightly as she sleeps.

You get up. Think you're getting up. Outside, it's completely dark. You forgot to close the shutters and you can see the moon, still up there, looking splendid and mocking you. This is the magical moment when those who have reasons to oppose this union must speak or forever hold their peace. You then turn towards her, the beloved, the sleeping one, the dead one. You have the impression that you are rediscovering something you lost a long time ago, something from your past, a series of blurred images, at the borders of unconsciousness, or perhaps a succession of forgotten words, words never uttered and which your open mouth attempts clumsily to reconstruct, but no sound is formed, and that which almost sprang forth again from the deepest part of you remains forever shrouded.

You take practically nothing, scarcely enough clothes to

be decent. Trousers, shirt, shoes. You leave the room and close the door softly behind you. You don't feel anything yet. Barely this fear of the dark, of the unforeseen. What's more, the liberated are always afraid. Silence in the corridor, on tiptoe. On the other hand, you go down the stairs rapidly. You arrive at the bottom. The lofty silence of cemeteries. Outside too, everything seems to be sleeping. Satisfied at last, the superb aspiration towards calm, towards iconoclastic silence! You walk through the streets with this haste that flees your thoughts, and you finally find the car. Don't think about anything. You drive off. In the darkness, it seems to you that your acceleration is like an unforeseen explosion.

Now you are on the motorway. You measure your monstrousness. But that's how it is. You don't want to talk. What's more, you realise that you're not suffering. I've always known that you were one of those people who don't know how to suffer, being one of those people who don't know how to love. You are driving fast now and you think back to what she said to you a few days ago, when she felt you were driving too fast: "Do you want to kill us or what?" It's now a done deed.

"It's over. Never again." These magic words echo in your head at one hundred and eighty kilometres per hour. You remember what you've experienced; you imagine what you could have experienced. And the tears that begin to appear are delicious. I've worked it out, Tristan. You never loved her. Never. But you are going to catch up with yourself. It's now that you're going to love her.

Believe me, you are going to begin to forget the truth. You always did prefer it lit up by bogus nostalgia. You are going to forget the terrifying void of your affair. You will retain only what is liable to move you. And these memories will form splendid circles and will spin, spin until you are drunk.

You will ceaselessly come back to that hotel room where you abandoned her. Always that moment of waking where her voice failed her: you weren't there any more! You imagine. Her unbrushed hair on her shoulders, that morning wildness that is for you the image of beauty. You are suffering with her, you say? You have to have a little heart to suffer. The truth is that, when you think of her, it's not of her but of yourself you're thinking. You're not weeping because you've lost her, but out of love for your handsome wounded face. Hers, moreover, you don't even see.

She is there, though, still sitting on the bed. She hasn't moved, she realised straight away. She got up to have a drink. Then she went onto the balcony. She didn't weep, this time, yet she has never felt so bad. It's not possible, she thinks. He's sure to come back! But she knows already. Will she go and rummage through your things? Perhaps she'll just want to take one of your shirts to press her face into it, your smell. I wouldn't even be surprised to learn that you left your things precisely for this image. Your suitcase, the red one. It's the irony of fate; but the fate of irony is the same hue. Inside, among your clothes, did she discover that ring that was to encircle her finger with promises? She will continue not to understand, there, somewhere. And, when evening comes, in the chasms of the ugliest kind of loneliness, the one that accompanies disillusionment, like her we will go to bed, thinking of the happiness we were expecting, but which will not come—just like sleep.

PHILIPPE BEAUSSANT

RENDEZVOUS
IN VENICE

Translated by Paul Buck and Catherine Petit

PIERRE THOUGHT HE KNEW his Uncle Charles well.
He had worked with him on a daily basis for fifteen years,
assisting the austere art historian in his studies. Yet five
years after Charles' death, Pierre finds a diary in which
his uncle had written of a secret, heartbreaking love affair.
When by chance Pierre meets Judith, the woman that his
uncle so passionately loved, neither one mentions the affair,
but the image that Pierre has of Charles is irrevocably
transformed. Then Pierre meets Judith's daughter, Sarah,
and soon finds that his own life will be changed forever.
Beaussant's superbly crafted narrative effortlessly conveys
the author's passion for art to the reader.

PHILIPPE BEAUSSANT is a novelist and musicologist.
He has written several works of fiction besides *Rendezvous in
Venice,* and is the author of numerous books on the history
and art of the Baroque era. He was awarded the *Brive Prix
de la Langue Francaise* in 2001 and the *Prix Littéraire du Prince
Pierre de Monaco* in 2004.

ISBN 1 901285 55 3 • 136 pp • £10.99

PUSHKIN PAPER

EDUARDO BERTI

AGUA

Translated by Alexander Cameron and Paul Buck
with an Afterword by Alberto Manguel

THE YEAR IS 1920, and Luis Agua, an authorised
representative of an electricity company arrives in Vila
Natal, an inhospitable village in Portugal. His objective
is to convince the inhabitants of the benefits of artificial
light. Before long Agua learns that the village and the castle
that presides over it hide deep secrets. A noble widow in
decline, a will that is both cruel and impertinent, a pioneer
of aviation, an epidemic and an unexpected ending; these
are the ingredients of this novel in which the themes of
love, revenge, humour, death and greed come together to
form an almost arithmetic narrative.

*"There is no doubt that Eduardo Berti must be considered one of the
most original, most accomplished novelists writing in Spanish today."*
ALBERTO MANGUEL

*"Eduardo Berti excites our fascination with storytelling ... His talent
and gracefulness are indisputable."* ANTÓN CASTRO

ISBN 1 901285 42 1 • 160 pp • £10/$14

UMBERTO PASTI
AGE OF
FLOWERS

Translated by Alastair McEwen

IN A WHITE CITY on the African shore of the Mediter-
ranean, Islamic fundamentalists are gaining control of the
streets and the European community of artists and deca-
dent aristocrats take refuge in memories and innumerable
vices. Luca and Irene, a young couple, are accepted into
the decaying and malicious ex-patriot society because of
Irene's family money.

On learning that his wife has breast cancer, Luca becomes
obsessed with the memory of his mother who died of the
same illness, and escapes into the only world in which he
feels secure, his garden. There he immerses himself ever
more deeply in his dream, becoming more and more like
the city's inhabitants who are rushing towards corruption
and destruction.

"A novel of subtlety and range."
MATTHEW WRIGHT TIMES LITERARY SUPPLEMENT

ISBN 1 901285 47 2 • 224 pp • £10/$14

PUSHKIN MODERN